# WOLF'S HEART

# MORE BY ANNE MARSH

# WOLF'S HEART

ANNE MARSH

## JACE

CUTE AS A BUTTON and sex on a stick shouldn't go together. Kind of like peanut butter and jelly with chocolate—either on its own is fucking great, but sticking them together is all kinds of wrong. The little werewolf parked on the other side of the desk somehow manages to be both cute and sexy at the same time. She makes me want to lick her. Makes me want to wrap her tight in my arms, hold her close, and get inside her every way I can.

Keelie Sue Berard doesn't want my feelings.

I've seen her at the Breed's clubhouse—seven times—and can't name one single time when she hasn't been trying to fade into the background. Keelie Sue doesn't like drawing attention to herself, but I can't look away from her.

The *cute* part is the way she's piled her hair on top of her head in some kind of messy twist anchored with a number two pencil. Wayward strands escape their captivity to brush around her cheeks, and I fight the urge to pet the soft skin beneath the curls. Lunging over the desk isn't nice, and I'm trying to turn over a new leaf where Keelie Sue is concerned.

Sort of.

*Sex on a stick* is where her blouse comes in. She must be going for office professional or some shit, because the blouse is a plain, utilitarian white. Kind of isn't the best color for her because it makes her look pale, but it's made out of some sort of silky fabric that clings to her boobs. Better yet, the front dips into a modest vee with a big-ass bow that plants right over the soft, sweet place between her breasts. Not that I can see more than the three inches of throat she's exposed, but I have a filthy imagination and I've spent way too much time mentally stripping Keelie Sue naked. Clearly, she has no idea that she's starring in my fantasies, because she proses on (and on) about receipts and P&Ls, waving a second pencil at the endless columns of numbers marching across her computer screen.

Fucking numbers.

Thirty-two years old and I can take apart a wolf with my bare hands, make him wish he's dead twice over and force him to acknowledge my domination. Instead, I'm sitting on an office chair, getting a lesson in first grade arithmetic. My inadequacies when it comes to adding and subtracting are one of several reasons why my challenging for Alpha seems like one of the worst fucking ideas I've had all year.

I already have a pack, and I'm number two wolf there. My brother is Alpha, and he rocks the leadership position. He sent me to infiltrate the Breed and get close to the top wolves. As far as I know, the Breed are the only wolf pack that is also a motorcycle club—and they get up to twice as much shit because of it.

Still, accepting a permanent place in the Breed pack feels like cheating on Cruz. Wolves move on, form their own packs or take their own territory, but Cruz and I are family and family matters.

"Any questions?" Keelie Sue's gaze darts away from the numbers on her screen, meets my own eyes briefly, then drops submissively. Apparently our lesson on the economics of running a ten-bay garage is over. Thank God.

"Got a couple," I drawl.

I drop my own gaze from Keelie Sue's pretty eyelashes (since she never lets me look at her for long, that's my usual view) to her throat. The pulse there beats fast and hard. I make her nervous.

Kind of want to change that.

If I become her Alpha, I'll be in charge of protecting her. Of making sure she has everything she needs and that she stays safe. Part of me—the part straining against my zipper—has definite ideas about how to accomplish that.

"Okay," she says, sounding more than a little scared.

Honestly, I'm not sure what has her panties in a twist. She's good at her job. I, on the other hand, am the moron who can't add—or remember to complete his paperwork. Who knew that running a werewolf pack came with forms? Fucking sucks, to be honest. I'm better suited to playing number two and bad cop.

Since she's already made her feelings for me clear—I'm the big bad wolf come to eat her up—I'm not feeling the incentive to behave. I shove out of my chair, stroll around her desk, and stop when my thighs bump against the back of her chair. She squeaks, and my dick gets harder. Not nice, but true. She's cute when she's flustered. She also turns this intriguing shade of pink that makes me wonder how far her blush extends... and that brings me back to my mental happy place of unbuttoning her blouse, stretching her out on her desk, and replacing all this boring-as-fuck paperwork with a little worshipping of Keelie Sue's sweet body and a whole lot of hot, nasty sex.

I set my hands on the back of her chair and let my fingers brush her shoulders. I can feel the heat of her through the thin fabric, and she smells good. Like flowers and sunlight, or something poetic like that. All I know is that I want to lick her from head to foot. Or from bottom to top—I'm flexible.

She sucks in a breath. Lets it out. See? That's cute right there, the way she tries to get control of herself. "Mr. Jones?"

I lean in closer, my mouth brushing her ear. Little pink pearls dangle from the lobe, and I tug gently. With my teeth. Isn't as if I can stop being a wolf, even for her. "When you call a guy Mister, you put ideas in his head."

"Really?" Her voice comes out a little shaky, but I don't think she minds my present position too much. Her body kind of melts into mine just a little, the straight line of her spine relaxing.

"Uh-huh," I growl and lick where I bit. "You got fantasies, Keelie Sue? Because I've got a few." I decide her little squeak means *tell me more, big guy* and since I feel downright helpful, I adjust my erection and tell her exactly what I'm thinking. "You call me *mister* and I start imagining I'm the boss in this office and you've been a bad, bad girl. Since you need to learn a lesson and I'm a giver, I'm gonna ease up that pretty skirt of yours and pull down your panties. Maybe I just look at you a bit, until you're wiggling and wanting more, and then I spank your butt pink."

Her face turns crimson, her hands clenching against the fabric of her skirt, working the neat lines into something less pristine. I've wrinkled her, and I love it.

"You think it's gonna hurt?" I brush my mouth against her ear, drinking in her shaky inhalation. "You're wrong. It may sting a little, but you're gonna love it. It's gonna feel so good you'll be arching up into my hand, wriggling like a little cat instead of the wolf you are. And then when we're perfectly clear about who's in charge in this office, I'll make you feel even better, and that's gonna take me kissing everywhere I spanked. So if you don't want me bringing those fantasies to life, maybe you should think about calling me Jace."

She hesitates, like she actually has to think about it, or maybe she's imagining me putting her over my knee and paddling her butt, because the sweetest scent of arousal teases me. Keelie Sue likes something about me all right, and her *like* makes me want to get closer. Hell, just let me get my fingers on her creaming pussy and I'll make her feel right about all this. About *me*.

"Jace," she whispers finally. The way she says my name tells me plenty. She'll call me whatever I want because I'm dominant and because, yeah, I turn her on. I want to push her, to chase her and drive myself in deep while she comes around me, milking my dick. Since *that* isn't happening, I need to get my shit together. The chase is fun, but I'm not into rape.

"See? That isn't so hard." I abandon the back of the chair and curl my fingers around her shoulders.

I have zero idea why I want to fuck her so badly. Sure, she's gorgeous and she has nice tits, but there are plenty of females with the same assets just waiting for me to walk into the clubhouse and pick them. It makes me sound like a cocksucking bastard thinking that, but those women and me? We know the sex is a transaction. They let me use their bodies, and I let them leverage my place in the club to get whatever it is they want. Power, revenge, drugs, a little cold hard cash… I understand those rules.

Keelie Sue, however, isn't in the rulebook.

Hell, she isn't in my league at all, and I'll be the first to admit it.

She's nice, she's smart, and the only thing I have to offer is dirty sex. If her daddy wasn't Big Red, she wouldn't get within a mile of the club. I might see her when I'm out riding and I might admire her rack, her ass, or her pretty face, but I'd keep on riding. I damned certain wouldn't stroke my fingers over the soft skin of her throat. Not the way I'm doing now.

"You had a question?" Her fingers flex on her thighs, and she stares down at them.

Yeah. I have a question all right, but I need to do this right. "What's it take for a wolf to get a date with you?"

## KEELIE SUE

I'm an accountant. Not a porn star or even reasonably sexy. The guys who come sniffing around me do so because dating the pack Alpha's daughter is generally considered the fast track to promotion. Provided, of course, you have the Alpha's permission. Otherwise, it's more of a death sentence. Guys don't want me for me—but apparently I've fallen down the rabbit hole, and in this alternate universe, adding and subtracting is the ultimate aphrodisiac. Or maybe Jace is just that bored.

It's possible. I haven't met a wolf who enjoys paperwork—which is why I'm usually safe in my office.

He rubs his fingers against the side of my throat lightly, the gesture strangely unthreatening. It's not like

I haven't spent my life around male werewolves—hello, my father is Alpha and I can shift—but this... is different. I expected Jace to be bossy, and sex is an excellent way to put a female in her place. The whole underneath-the-guy-and-taking-orders thing makes it clear who's in charge, and Jace is one hundred percent dominant. If he wasn't, my dad wouldn't try so hard to make him commit to our pack.

His fingers move, stroking my skin.

And it isn't bad.

It really, really isn't. He's careful and while he's in my space, he isn't exactly a ravaging beast. If he didn't make me so nervous, I might enjoy the simple touch. Wolves love touching, and my wolf misses the casual skin-to-skin contact of friends and lovers. She's drinking this up.

Long-term, however, I doubt he'll be content to brush the pads of his fingertips over the few inches of exposed skin on my throat. He'll want more, and he's out of my league. He's a brutal enforcer and a lethal fighter, and I'm safest far, far away from him. The little spark of pleasure from the way he touches me is fantastic, but doing anything more is like French-kissing a powder keg. Jace won't mean to hurt me, but guys like him—let's just say that our relationship only has two possible endings. Either he walks out my door and I get on with my life, or he hurts me.

"Keelie Sue?" He says my name in a deep, raspy voice, and I actually get wet on the spot. That's never happened before, and I don't know whether I should be mortified or do a happy dance around my office. Apparently I'm not totally screwed up by my sex life. Yay, me.

"What?" I ask him, trying to sort out what I feel. I don't really want to have sex with him, so I need to be careful. I'm just the accountant who's filled him in on how the pack's profit margins work and where he needs to step up his game. Jace is truly terrible with paperwork. I don't know if he just can't be bothered or if he has some other, larger problem, but the receipts he brought me make no sense. He's supposed to purchase parts for the pack-run garage, but the receipts don't match the cash outlays, and he spent *more* than he took out. So he's not thieving—and honestly, theft is the last thing I'd expect from him anyhow, like the zombie apocalypse and/or my dad inviting me to retire to a blissfully pack-free Bora Bora—but I have no clue what he's up to.

"I'm asking you out on a date," he tells me, sounding amused. Somehow, impossibly, he moves closer, and his leg brushes my arm. I fight the urge to leap out of my chair. It's not like I can go anywhere—and male wolves love to chase. If I bolt, he might decide I'm his new favorite squeaky toy.

Most wolves break their toys.

"Uh," I say, sounding as inarticulate as I feel. Approximately a million questions run through my head, starting with *Why do you really want to do this?* And *Did my dad approve?* I'm not stupid enough to date without parental approval, even if I am twenty-one. That's yet another drawback to being the Alpha's daughter.

He steps back and spins me around in my chair so that I face him. My new position is no improvement, because now I can't possibly ignore just how much of Jace there is—including the very impressive bulge in his jeans. Apparently numbers do indeed turn him on. I guess there's no accounting for taste. Heh.

He eyes me, his face giving away nothing. Then he nods as if he's come to a decision and crouches down so that he's on eye level with me. Carefully he places his hands flat and loose on his thighs. Without him looming over me I feel less trapped, and my wolf relaxes.

"I'm not gonna eat you up," he growls, and the

12

words sound almost... affectionate? I have to be hallucinating. Next I'll be expecting candy hearts and roses when most werewolves are more likely to bring me a fresh, hot kill and then press for sex.

After a hunt, when their blood is up, that's when it's most dangerous to be a pack female. Mating is usually a permanent relationship, and my dad is all for it if he gets to pick the pairs, but casual sex is also a given. I don't like hookups, and I try to avoid the clubhouse whenever I can, especially when the pack has been hunting, but there were a few nights when I failed...

A big finger taps me lightly on the nose, and my wolf whines.

"You gonna come back to me?" Jace doesn't sound pissed about my daydreaming. In fact, he seems more amused than anything. I guess it's good he has a sense of humor.

"What are you thinking about?" I ask, figuring that's my safest response.

He ducks his own head so he can look into my eyes. "I'm thinking about kissing you. You want a test run, Keelie Sue? See how our date could end?"

A downright sinful smile curves his gorgeous mouth, softening the harsh lines of his face. I drop my gaze and stare at the tribal tattoos inked into his forearms. He has a playful side, and it's unexpected. I feel his sigh brush over my skin, and my answer flies out of my mouth before I can think it through. I blame my wolf. "Yes. Please."

"I like the way you say *please*," he says roughly and then he leans forward. His mouth captures mine, his tongue stroking carefully along the crease of my lips. He presses lightly, and I obey his unspoken command and open up for him. He makes a harsher, hungrier noise, a primitive sound that thrills me as much as it frightens me.

He kisses me and I lean into him, deepening the connection in the one place we touch. His tongue explores me, and I'm startled to discover that I like this kiss. He moves closer, edging between my knees and planting his hands on either side of my hips. His thumbs trace a little pattern on my hips, soothing and yet feeding my hunger for him. *Sweet* and *gentle* aren't words I've ever even thought about in the same sentence as Jace. But he is.

This is crazy.

I have my dad's favorite wolf between my knees, my body straining toward his, and I wouldn't mind taking this further. Jace has to know it, too. He can smell my arousal—there's no hiding it. But... anyone could walk in, and word would get straight back to my dad. I don't think he'll mind, but I can't afford to take the chance. Worse, if my dad likes the idea of my hooking up with Jace, he'll give us his blessing and that will be the end of my single status and any hope of freedom.

I jerk back. "We need to stop," I whisper, doing my best to ignore the delicious, needy ache in my pussy. I want what I can't have, but I'm used to that. "This isn't a good idea."

He strokes his thumb over my hip in a lazy, warm circle. "Let me."

It would be so, so easy to *let* him, and I'd enjoy every wicked minute.

"No." I hold my breath, waiting for the explosion. For the anger.

Jace gives me a speculative look, then shoves to his feet and strides to the door. "Think about that date," he says.

A few seconds later I hear the sound of a bike's pipes tearing away.

2

## KEELIE SUE

S HOOT. A PARTY ROCKS the clubhouse tonight. A
sea of Harleys fills the parking lot outside the
warehouse the Breed claimed years ago as their property. Three prospects—two humans, one wolf—patrol
the lines of bikes, keeping an eye on things. As if anyone in this rundown, shit-out-of-luck neighborhood
would be dumb enough to touch so much as a hubcap
belonging to the Breed. My father's motorcycle club
has reigned supreme here for the past five years, controlling the flow of illegal arms, dirty money, and even
more illegal drugs in and out of this portion of Baton
Rouge.

The Breed's home turf in Baton Rouge is part
warehouse, part fortified bunker. When the werewolf
club isn't terrorizing Baton Rouge in lupine form, the
members ride Harleys and rule over the local human
gangs in two-legged form. Either way, the men inside

the clubhouse are bad news. They drink, they fight, and they run an illegal arms and drug trade that spilled into the streets months ago.

There isn't much Big Red won't do—or order someone else to do. When I can, I keep my head down and stay out of things. Walking away isn't an option. Big Red is a mean bastard, and being his daughter doesn't give me a free pass. I'm his weapon, his negotiating chip, and when he's had too much to drink and his day hasn't gone according to plan, I'm his punching bag. If I wasn't a wolf and therefore a quick healer, I'd be dead by now. I also negotiated six months ago for my own apartment, and the separate space helps too.

Tonight, however, looks like a *bargaining chip* kind of night. He ordered me to show up at the clubhouse and then sent over clothes like I was his own personal Barbie doll. The command wardrobe means I'm not in my usual uniform of business skirt and blouse. Good thing I know how to ignore what I can't change, because I've traded sensible pumps and nylons for three-inch stilettos and fishnet stockings. My leather mini-skirt barely covers my butt, and the tank top is low enough to show more than a hint of the red Victoria's Secret hiding beneath. I look like one of the pass-arounds the MC members fuck and forget. Yay, me. The *forget* part works for me, but the *fuck*? Not so much.

The last time my dad picked out what I wore, it turned out to be my wedding day. Since I've struck that day from my mind, I keep my head down and concentrate on the warehouse, the party, and getting inside.

Halfway to the door, the wolf prospect steps in front of me, body checking me. "You got an invitation, baby girl?"

Fang is big. Aggression radiates off him, and my wolf immediately has me taking a step back. He laughs like we're playing a game, and slaps a hand on my butt, squeezing hard. I'm not proud of the little squeak that flies out of my throat. I'd like to be stronger. More kickass. Less me. Still, even though I'm not Wonder Woman, the wolf's hand shoots off my butt.

"Keelie Sue?" When he growls my name, I nod. Apparently he recognizes my voice. Or the top of my head, my cleavage, or even my butt. "Fuck."

*Over my dead body.*

My life sucks, but I intend to change that.

I lift my head, pinching the edge of my skirt between two fingers and rubbing the soft leather. "Dad texted me."

*Don't sound scared.* There isn't much I can do about my scent, but my voice and my hands are a different story. No tremor, no tell. Just sweet little me. That sometimes works for me.

My mind heads straight to my last mating night, and I force the memories back. This wolf will eat me alive, and I'm not sure that's even a euphemism. The rumors about Fang's sexual preferences are disturbing.

"You go on in, baby girl," he says, stepping back. "Make sure you tell your daddy that I said hi." As soon as he's patched into the club, he'll be after me. He reeks of ambition, and I'm a shortcut to the top of the pack's pecking order. The thought of hooking up with Fang is so awful that I scuttle past him even faster than usual and he laughs. He knows I'm scared, and he likes it.

That's not tonight's problem though so I go inside. Humans and werewolves pack the warehouse. The Breed has a membership of some forty wolves, and almost the same number of humans. There are also dozens of prospects, both shifters and not, who hope to become full members and be patched into the club. They do whatever the club's members tell them, kind of like a combination of unpaid servants and indentured hit men. The only women here are for either serving beer or sex.

Locating my dad is easy. He holds court in the middle of the warehouse, near the bar. He sprawls in a banquette raised above everyone else, surrounded by his usual posse of mean, hard-edged wolves. I don't spot Jace and that's the one bright spot in my evening.

Seeing Jace here would be the cherry on my shit sundae. Complicated doesn't begin to describe my feelings for that wolf. Not only is he the biggest wolf I've ever laid eyes on, but that oversized body of his doesn't come with a single nice bone. He's crude. He has no filter. And he doesn't give a fuck. He makes that perfectly clear each time I interact with him.

I was too glad to escape from our paperwork encounter yesterday, even if *escape* is a temporary fiction and the more accurate words are *fallback*, *retreat*, and *wait for shit to hit the fan again*. Avoiding Jace forever is impossible.

Not only is my wolf nemesis the best fighter this pack has ever had, but my old man is desperate to win his loyalty since technically Jace still runs with the Jones pack despite having patched into Breed MC. He swore an oath of loyalty to the bikers, but the wolves are still a big question mark. Winning him away from the Jones clan would be a coup. The Jones Alpha busted several of our wolves, and I suspect my dad is looking for a little tit-for-tat by taking Jace. I sure as heck don't know why he trusts the wolf given his family loyalties.

The party happening inside the warehouse definitely looks like Jace's kind of scene, making his absence all the more remarkable. The Breed are not a classy lot. The bar does a brisk business, as do the beer kegs set up on one edge of the room. The dress code is motorcycle boots, blue jeans, and leather kuttes. Accessories include bruises, scars, chains, and enough weaponry to fill a National Guard armory. The guys take their right to bear arms seriously.

The only thing that seems to distract them from drinking and combat stories is sex. Even though the night is still young, several wolves are already mounting the pass-around girls. I've never understood what makes a woman decide that her aim in life includes being a motorcycle groupie. Rough sex doesn't begin to cover the way the wolves go at them. I let my gaze slide over two wolves screwing themselves into a worn-out woman sprawled on a pool table. The sounds coming out of her mouth are more shrieks than moans.

I keep on walking. I know better than to interrupt or register a protest. She has to do that for herself, same way I'm the only one who can stand up to my dad for me. Angry tears prick my eyelids. I want to be anywhere but here, but I come to a stop in front of my dad.

"'Bout time you got here," he snaps.

Funny. I came as soon as I got his message, and since he employs me to manage the club's books, he knows precisely where to find me. Since there's no good answer, I keep my mouth shut and my head down. *Don't challenge him. Don't look him in the eye.*

I'm hardly seen as a credible threat here. More than one set of hard eyes moves over me, assessing then dismissing me like dear old dad does. I lack claws, teeth, and visible firearms, which makes me a non-threat in the wolves' eyes and which just goes to show that men underestimate women all the time. The ability to shift doesn't make them any smarter.

"I'm picking you a new mate." My dad drops his bombshell with about as much interest as if he's discussing the weather. Maybe less, frankly, because I'm a sure thing in his world. Then he dismisses me and turns to his lieutenant and officers. No details, no explanation, no nothing—and since wolves mate for life,

I need more. Including an escape route.

"No." The word doesn't come out very loudly, but it comes out. That counts for something, I promise myself. Those two letters, that one word? *Count* for something. Next time I'll scream the word. Next time I'll *make* him listen. Baby steps.

"Jesus." My dad turns back to me, his fist swinging my way so fast I don't see it coming. I feel each knuckle meet my cheekbone though. The impact knocks me off my feet and drives me into the floor. Pain splinters through my face as I fight to breathe. I wish I could say I'm not frightened. That I bounce to my feet, spit in his face, and kick him in the balls. Do *something*. Just like always though, my wolf takes over and I curl into a ball, whimpering. He's Alpha. I'm Beta. The scents of his other wolves surround me, reminding me that they're bigger, stronger. *Meaner*.

Tonight will hurt so bad.

He cocks his head and looks down at me. The toe of his boot nudges my ribs hard. "I'm holding a mating ball next week to celebrate your new pairing."

A *ball*. Like he's fancy and he's proposing one of those black-tie charity affairs where the people come in limousines with their checkbooks in one hand and a flute of champagne in the other. This will be a bonfire and kegger deep in the bayou, and it will also be no-holds-barred drugs, drinking, and a side of violence. The mating bond doesn't have to be romantic and it doesn't always form an intimate connection between the two wolves involved, but it always involves sex. Lots and lots of sex—and my dad's wolves won't care if it's consensual or not. Speaking up with my dad's boot banging on my ribs, however, isn't happening.

And then he puts the nail in the coffin anyway. "Got us a whole bunch of human girls too," he tells me, like I should freaking applaud him or be grateful for the company.

A grin splits the face of his lieutenant, a big, mean-eyed shifter with a scar bisecting his cheek. Not much makes Gator smile. Fast cars, new weapons, and the opportunity to dish out a world of hurt tops the man's list. He earned his name after he fell into the bayou late one night, and a particularly vicious fifteen-foot alligator decided he'd make a good midnight snack. Gator carved his attacker up—with his teeth—and then made himself a new pair of boots. He's never touched me, but I've caught him watching me more than once. Gator is hard to figure out.

"Some of them are really pretty too," Gator drawls. "Gonna have a beauty contest and keep us the winners for mates."

There are no winners in this scenario.

"How many girls you got?" It's not like I want to make conversation about this, but I need to know. Because you know how everyone has that line they won't cross? Human trafficking is apparently mine. I have no idea how to fix this, but I'm going to try. I don't even know where they keep the girls, which is another thing I add to my mental list of crap to worry about.

"You concerned about the competition? Don't be." My dad's boot makes contact again, and my ribs protest. "I'm gonna mate you to the strongest wolf there is."

*God, no.* My stomach joins the rest of me on the floor, a sickening, too-familiar plunge. Memories tug at me, horrible, awful snippets from the last time my dad mated me to one of his wolves. I emerged from *that* night a widow—and I'm pretty sure I won't be that lucky twice in a row. Bolt's death was accidental, but I'd have done it on purpose too and that's the truth.

"You got something else to say to me, baby girl?" My dad pokes me harder in the ribs with his boot. The sharp blossom of pain almost drowns out the unwelcome sensations liquefying my insides.

Nothing's gone right tonight. I'd like to pretend that I could get up and walk out, but truth is, there's nowhere I can run where the Breed can't find me. I tried it once, after Bolt's death, and they about killed me. And since there's no point in making useless stands, I've bided my time ever since. Someday, somebody will make a mistake and hand me my opportunity. I just have to wait it out, hold on long enough.

But daddy dearest isn't done with me. Another hard smack drives my head backward into the floor. I'm still seeing stars when he hoists me up onto his table. Glasses fly, and his wolves holler in appreciation. Just once, I want a happily-ever-after ending. Something upbeat and less like one of those Russian novels where everybody dies or gets banished to Siberia to freeze to death in a snowstorm.

"I'm goin' to do you a favor, baby girl." His words whisper harshly in my ear, so low that no one else can catch them. "Bolt was a damned unlucky wolf, and I've had my doubts that *luck* was involved with his death."

Denial. Denial is my best friend here. I was truly alone in the bayou when Bolt met his end, and I knew then that I had to keep what happened a secret. "I had nothing to do with that," I croak out.

"Might not mind if you did," my dad says, surprising me. Or maybe not. As long as I'm single—even if I'm branded a black widow—he can mate me to a new wolf of his choosing. As long as I'm mateless, I'm all his to control. "I've got my eye on Jace Jones."

Guess Jace's interest in me the other day wasn't so benevolent after all—he probably knew this night was coming.

"Why?" The word fly out of my mouth before I can bite it back. *Stupid.* I might as well dance a cancan dressed in scarlet in a bullring. My dad doesn't allow questions.

"He's one tough son-of-a-bitch," he growls against

my ear, shifting just enough that his teeth prick my vulnerable skin. Big Red is one of the few wolves in the pack that can manage a partial shift. The ability means he's strong, but it also makes him mean. I about pee myself when his canines scrape my ear, and then he bites down and I scream.

## JACE

The Breed pack needs new management. If I hadn't promised my brother Cruz that I'd keep my head down and focus on gathering the intel he needs to take the club down in the human law courts, I'd do some housecleaning. Big Red is a mean son-of-a-bitch, ruling the pack through terror and intimidation, even though a smarter wolf would know that any loyalty bought with pain isn't worth shit.

I can take him in a fight.

The current Alpha knows it too, because he's pussy-footed around me, sounding me out and seeing how much of his crap I'll take. He needs to know if I'm gonna challenge him, or if I'm less ambitious and will be content to take his orders and be number two. I'm not Alpha of the Year material, but Big Red is into some nasty stuff, and averting my eyes doesn't sit right with me. The man practically begs for a beatdown, and I'm the only wolf strong enough to deliver it. Kinda makes it my job, the way I see it.

When I enter the clubhouse, Big Red is in the process of vaulting up onto the bar, kicking a rack of glasses out of the way in a shower of glass and noise. Nice. As soon as he has the attention of every wolf in the place, he reaches down and hauls something—make that *someone*—off the floor. Place is fucking nasty too, because housecleaning isn't something Big Red bothers with. Not that I'd do it myself, but there are cleaning crews for that kind of shit. Cash fixes some problems.

"Who wants to mate my girlie?" The asshole straightens up and bellows the question loud enough for the entire club to hear. He gives the girl he's hanging onto a shake, knocking the hair back from her bruised face.

Ah, fuck.

Guess there's gonna be a change in management tonight after all.

Keelie Sue is a sweetheart and she deserves way better than the asshole worrying her. Mentally I root for her to come up swinging, maybe nail the bastard in the balls. She can do it too, because Big Red underestimates her and that gives her an advantage. Keelie Sue has fight in her, but she hides it well. She's a watcher, and she doesn't jump into a fight or come out swinging first. She's more like one of those medieval Italian ladies—a Borgia princess through and through. Piss her off and she just might poison you. Big Red doesn't look worried, but I've heard the stories about how when Keelie Sue's first mate disappeared, some people thought she had a hand in it.

I hope she did it.

Or maybe I'm being overly optimistic. Don't think I have it in me, but it's possible. Because whenever I see her, she stinks of terror. She's a Beta, her daddy has anger management issues, and she's already been mated to the one asshole wolf. And despite the mysterious end of that union, I don't care who or what turned the guy into gator bait, because when I do the math, Keelie Sue couldn't have been much more than sixteen when her daddy paired her off.

Asshole got what he had coming to him.

She doesn't look too young tonight, however. More like she's seen inside my head and dressed to match last night's wet dream. I'm a bastard for appreciating her curvy, bare legs, but I'm not dead, and my dick doesn't always take orders from my head. Usually Keelie Sue walks around in something that looks hand-picked from her momma's closet—her sixty-something, church-going, I'm-gonna-cover-it-up momma. Doesn't take a genius to figure out her secret plan involves fading into the woodwork until all the badass wolves forget she's there. Tonight, however, her plan has failed spectacularly. She's all gussied up in a leather miniskirt and a teeny-tiny black tank top. The skirt has worked halfway up her ass, and her pretty, red panties match the bra peeking out of her top. I want to wrap her up in my arms and get her out of there.

*Freedom.* Her silent demand is right there in the hate-filled gaze she turns on the room watching her daddy throw her around. Maybe she'll let me take out her old man, but that's all she wants from me.

Fuck, some white knight I am. She claws at the hand holding her aloft, where the bastard is using her ponytail for fucking leverage. Nah. I'm not walking away from this fight. I vault across the room like I'm some kinda fucking flying machine.

"She's mine," I growl, trying to dial my aggression back. Kill Big Red, and then Cruz and I will have words. He'll demand *evidence* and dead guys don't produce that. Problem is, I'm not lying when I claim Keelie Sue. Some primal piece of me has already decided I'll be the last man she fucks. Might not be her first, but I'll be her best, and that starts with my getting her asshole father off her back.

"Not yet," Big Red says. He laughs, a mean, knowing bark. "Not until I say so."

Christ.

Another quick glance at Keelie Sue tells me she doesn't like the word choice, but is in no position to protest. I could cut her free—won't take much. One flick of my wrist, and I can send my hunting knife clean through that ponytail of hers. Since she probably won't thank me for the haircut, I give using my words another shot.

"Not something I want to talk about," I admit. Look at me telling the truth tonight. "So how about you just hand her over, and we call it quits for the night?"

Big Red flips me a *fuck you* with his free hand. "I don't need you talking, boy."

"You gonna give me a hint?" My eyes flick to Keelie Sue. It's business as usual with her. I don't have the faintest clue what she wants from me.

"Wolf who breeds Keelie Sue for me gets to be my first lieutenant." Big Red doesn't dress it up, just lays the offer out there, and shit, even I can tell it plays well with the other wolves in the room. No need to challenge the old man—just take the daughter, knock her up, and claim it all someday in the glorious future when Big Red bites it and goes to the happy hunting ground in the sky (or heads down to a hotter, more hellish place). It's a payday without the work week, and too many of the Breed wolves are lazy sons-of-bitches.

"Do I look like a portable sperm bank to you?" I prowl closer and slap my hand on the bar. Me down here, him up there. It isn't a position I favor. I consider my options. Some of the other wolves press closer, their shoulders banging into mine as they set their hands on the bar. Keelie Sue whimpers, kind of like she's about to really lose it, and I plant my boots on the nasty-ass floor. She should know I won't let these other fuckers have a taste of her. Bad enough that they can all see up her skirt and look at that red thong of hers. Unfortunately, *should* doesn't mean that she does, which means I'll just have to show her.

"That's right." Big Red adjusts his grip on Keelie Sue, hauling her up against him and jerking her head up when she tries to duck her face into her arm. *My girl needs to kick the man in the balls, because hiding won't work.* "You got to earn it, boy."

I'm no one's *boy*. I might be part man, but I'm part wolf too, and the wolf part of me stands more than ready to claim its territory, starting with Keelie Sue. The calculation in Big Red's eyes is plain to see. I don't know what the bastard has planned or hopes for, but I'll shoot him down and it will be a fucking pleasure. I definitely want to watch the guy bleed.

"I should let someone have a taste of her tonight," he announces, like he's passing around a rack of ribs or a bottle of Gentleman Jack. *Now I'm gonna make killing him slow.* The wolves around me growl, the pheromones rolling off them. *Oui.* They want their taste, but it happens over my dead body.

Keelie Sue is mine.

She doesn't know it, she doesn't want it, but neither of those two conditions change a goddamned thing.

"Or I could give my baby girl a fighting chance," he drawls. Not sure who freezes faster, me or Keelie Sue. She wants an out, and I can practically feel her hoping Big Red isn't just messing with her. "If she gets to the door, she's off the hook tonight. Otherwise, whoever catches her can keep her—for tonight. I'm gonna give you all a chance to see what you'd be getting if you mated with my Keelie Sue. What do you say, honey?"

He yanks Keelie Sue's head up so she has to look him in the eye. Not like she can nod with the death grip he has on her hair, but she gives it a shot.

Because he's a troublemaking bastard, Big Red tosses her into the air—away from me. Everything goes slo-mo for a moment. She shrieks, not so quiet now, and flails her arms and legs like maybe she can fly. That little miniskirt of hers doesn't come with a parachute though, and she's about to ass-plant it on the floor. She has enough bruises. She doesn't need more.

Getting there in time to catch her isn't an option even if I'd trade my left nut to make it. Instead, I concentrate on what I can do. Which is take down the eight wolves racing for her. Keelie Sue may be a Beta wolf, but she isn't stupid. She'll run as soon as she picks herself up off the floor. All I have to do is hurt the assholes chasing her, and then she'll be all mine. No way she outruns me.

I don't even bother shifting, just lay into the wolves around me, and damned if my heart isn't beating out some kind of primal rhythm while I snap bones and deal out a world of hurt. *Mine.*

Kinda says it all.

3

## KEELIE SUE

I TAKE THE RUNNING start my dad offers and tear for the door. My knees burn and my eyes water, but I have exactly one chance to make it outside. Outside, maybe I can lose myself in the streets, or find a safe place to shift. I'm faster on four legs, but the change hurts like hell and leaves me vulnerable. It certainly isn't something I can do now.

The door gets closer, and for a moment I think I might actually make it. Pulling on everything I have, I force my legs to move faster. Dad's throwdown ended with my skirt rucked up around my waist, but I'm not stopping to fix that particular problem now. I sprint and weave around the partygoers. The smell of spilled beer and leather fills my nose; growls fill the air behind me. I know what's happening. Turning to look will only slow me down, so I mentally fill in the details. The wolves are fighting over me, and the biggest, meanest SOB will beat down the others and then he'll come for me.

Unless I make it out the door first.

That's my dad's deal. Honestly, I'm not sure he'll honor it, but it's the only shot I have right now. Reach my car, and I buy myself some time. Not enough, not forever, because those aren't the rules of Big Red's game, but maybe I can avoid being some wolf's taster course tonight. *Please.*

A hard arm snakes around my waist, pulling me back against a muscled body and killing my hopes of a getaway. Since I'm looking down to watch my feet, I get a good look at the Celtic-looking tattoo scrolled across the guy's forearm. Could be Pict for asshole-of-the-century for all I know, but the bold, black lines suit Jace. Problem is, he doesn't suit *me*.

"Stop fighting me, sweetheart." Jace's voice makes my wolf quiver. If voices were flavors, his would be caramel and bourbon, and it makes me think about licking him from head to foot. My wolf whimpers again, not convinced that *licking* is our safest plan. The man radiates danger, and putting more space between us is even more attractive. When I try to pull away, however, Jace squeezes, and what air remains in my lungs promptly takes a vacation.

"I'll take that as a no," he grunts, and then he lifts me over his shoulder like he's a damned caveman. Funny how the position has always struck me as kind of sexy in books. In reality, his shoulder is hard and digs into my stomach in a way that's both nauseating and uncomfortable at the same time. When I try to push up, he holds me in place with one big hand cupping my butt. If he slides his fingers a few inches lower, he'll touch me. *His* big fingers on *my* bare skin… because he hasn't even had the decency to tweak my skirt back into place, and I plan on holding that omission against him.

I lift my head, and spot the pile of bodies. Shoot. Jace doesn't mess around. I count at least five wolves sprawled on the floor. Big Red stands on top of the bar watching us leave. He looks mean as a snake, his arms folded across his chest.

"When you take her, you think about taking your place as my second," Big Red hollers. I've never heard the word *please* cross the man's lips, and he clearly has no plans to acquire manners tonight.

Jace doesn't break step, just raises his hand and gives my father the middle-finger salute. Apparently there is something about the man that I like after all. I'd echo his gesture, but I'm not feeling that suicidal.

Jace carries me out into the parking lot and makes for a row of bikes. He squeezes my butt, and I don't know how I feel about that. I really don't. "You gonna struggle?"

Guess that depends. "You *gonna* hurt me?"

## JACE

Keelie Sue's conversational bombshell sums up our relationship. She expects the worst from me, but what she hasn't figured out is that I have zero desire to go at her with my fists or any other weapon. My dick is another story, but that chapter can wait.

I set her on her feet while I consider my answer. Must be taking too long, because she tries to back away from me. Since I have my hand around her wrist, she doesn't get far.

"Guess you're stuck with me," I point out finally. Probably should sell her on my good points—or hell, try for a kiss—but we both know I'm no fucking prize.

"You could just take me home," she points out hopefully. "And take a pass on the mating claim."

Her eagerness to be rid of me sucks. When I stopped by her office yesterday, I was thinking dinner and a movie. She's cute, she's single, so why not have a little fun? She, on the other hand, was industriously working through paperwork and apparently didn't know shit about her dad's mating intentions until he bellowed them to the entire clubhouse tonight. I can't blame her for not being on board with his plan. If someone tried to pass me around like a party favor, I'd rip the guy's goddamned head off.

The way she stinks of fear right now goes in the negative column, however. I don't want her scared of me. Not sure what I want, to be honest, but fear definitely isn't on the mental list I'm keeping.

"Look. We got a problem," I snap. "I need you on this bike, and we need to get out of here."

"And I need to live my own life," she spits right back. Then she ducks her head, her hair falling over her face, like her sass surprised her. She's lost that pretty ponytail she sported earlier. I kinda liked the way the long tail flicked over her shoulders as she bounced through the crowd of wolves. Of course, I've also fantasized more than once about fisting her hair, dragging her head back for my kiss as I fuck inside her body. Once again? I'm not nice.

Which in no way explains what I do next. I let go of her. She can come with me—or not. Lady's choice. I straddle the bike and turn it on. The engine's roar echoes off the buildings, nothing subtle about the blast of sound.

She hovers there on the sidewalk like she thinks maybe I'm playing games with her. Could have told her I'm no fucking cat to play with my prey, but I'm not in the mood to make things easier for her. I do give her the truth, though.

"The other wolves are gonna come on out here. You can ride with me, or you can stay here and pick out a new mate."

Her eyes flick back to the clubhouse. "You didn't kill them?"

Can't tell if I've disappointed her or not—I should probably get clear on that point soon, because I'm betting on similar opportunities arising in my future and it's good to know her limits. I have zero problems killing asshole wolves, but females can be soft about those things.

"Waste not, want not," I say lightly and pat the seat behind me. I can force her, but it will be a pain in the ass, and it's not how I want our relationship to go. And... rewind. Am I thinking about Keelie Sue in *relationship* terms? Because yesterday my feelings didn't go beyond popcorn and a flick, or so I thought.

"You don't want to be my mate," she announces, but she sounds more hopeful than certain. "I suck at sex, and there are prettier women inside."

"I'll make do," I promise her, although the hopeful note in her voice kinda makes me snort. She isn't getting off that easy. Not tonight. Her body is a pretty package and her mouth plants dirty thoughts in my head about guiding her lips to my dick—and then giving her a few suggestions. Hell, I want to tongue her, lick everywhere she's covered up. She's my fucking Christmas present, gift wrapped by the pack, and I want to open her up. Honestly, I'd crawl inside her if I could, because she feels that right to me and I've survived this long by listening to my instincts. The only thing standing between her and getting spread on top of the nearest pool table is her daddy.

And me.

Clearly, she doesn't want me either, but I'm not letting her get hurt. Have a few suspicions of my own that I'm too little, too late in that department, but I'm here now and I'm not going anywhere.

"Hop on," I repeat.

She doesn't move from her post on the sidewalk. "I have a car."

I know what she drives. Her car is a POS import with more miles on it than one of the club's pass-arounds. Outrunning it won't be hard—and that's if it even starts.

"You're asking for a spanking," I growl. "Stop making shit so hard."

I don't even mean my dick, but that particular part of me throbs in violent agreement and damned if Keelie Sue doesn't get wet. I inhale sharply and her sweet scent wraps itself around me. Keelie Sue gets wet thinking about my spanking her. That's fan-fucking-tastic because I'm absolutely in the mood to oblige her.

"I'll have someone bring your car by your place." I pat the bike's seat again, harder than is necessary. She jumps at the short, loud slap and I wonder if we're both imagining that was my hand on her ass. "Now hop on unless you want that spanking right here in front of Fang."

That earns me another squeak and she bites her bottom lip, her teeth worrying the soft skin. I'm definitely a bastard, because I want to replace her teeth with mine. Want to kiss her, want to take her mouth. And that's only the start. My shortcomings can be summed up in three words: I'm not enough. I know that. She has to know it too. In fact, we're perfectly clear on that particular point but... Christ. What now? We're not really gonna get it on in the parking lot with half the club gunning for her, so why isn't she on my bike already?

"I can't ride a bike in this skirt," she admits in a small voice.

Naturally I look. She's twitched the fabric down at

some point, which isn't an improvement to my mind, but even so there wasn't much for her to work with. The skirt barely skims the tops of her thighs. The moment she straddles the bike, the tiny scrap of leather will make like a belt and hug her waist. It damned certain isn't gonna give her any protection on our ride. A stray pebble, a little wind...

Fuck.

I don't want her hurting. I rummage around in my saddlebags and slap a pair of sweatpants in her hands. Good thing I went to the gym earlier.

"Ten seconds," I warn her. After that, I don't care what she wears. She gets on the bike, and we get out of here. I settle back on the bike to wait. And count.

She gets the message, because she doesn't argue. She steps into my sweats and shimmies them up. Even blushing like a virgin, she's cute as hell. I also get another flash of her red thong, which is all the incentive I need to reach out and pull her onto my bike. Pass her a helmet too, because safety first. It doesn't matter that the prospects watch us, that I'm playing into her old man's hands, or that driving off with her is tantamount to breaking with my brother's pack. Somehow I can't bring myself to leave her stranded at the club knowing that Big Red's lieutenants will fight for a piece of her ass and she'll get hurt in the process.

I gun the bike, feeling pissy. No one puts his hands on my Keelie Sue, but keeping her hasn't been part of the plan either. But now I have her on my bike, and there isn't a whole lot of space between us. Sharing a seat kinda forces her to slide forward, her pussy planting against my ass, and that move doesn't make getting out of here any easier. My dick about punches through the front of my jeans; it's that eager for me to turn around and drive myself into her.

*Gotta stop thinking like that.*

"You fall off, and I might not stop." As if.

35

She must believe me because she slides her hands beneath my jacket and around my waist. Her fingers are cold as shit, and she's lost her shoes. Her torn-up nylons peek out of the cuffs of my sweatpants. Some protector I am. She doesn't want anything to do with me, but I can't overlook the obvious. Sliding my leather jacket off, I drop it into her lap with a shrug. Isn't hard to do given our proximity.

"Put it on." Not much I can do about her feet right now. My boots would fall off her, and even I know dirty gym socks aren't romantic. Although fuck romantic. I just need to get her out of here and somewhere safer. Then we'll sort this mess out, figure out what she needs. If I'm lucky, it's hot, dirty sex and a spanking game.

She hesitates, then obeys. Makes me wonder what else she'll do and how far she'll let me push her. As soon as she has the jacket on and her arms back around my waist, I put the bike in neutral. I suspect it's not, in fact, my lucky night, but my dick leaps like it really thinks we're riding off for a night of rough sex.

It's gonna have to get used to the disappointment.

"You ready?" Not like I'll let her leave, but still. I really don't want her face-planting on the gravel. She squeaks something I decide to take as agreement. Honestly? I'd like to interpret the sound as a *fuck me, please*, but that isn't my big head talking. I hit the mental mute button.

Fang, the prospect guarding the bikes, ambles over when we approach the exit, and I slow the bike. Not like we're breaking speed records, but I've got an idea.

"Keys," I grunt to Keelie Sue.

She fishes in a pocket, produces a set of car keys, and stretches out her hand toward Fang. Instead of just grabbing the keys from her, the bastard tightens his fingers on hers, and that has me growling again. Not my fault I don't like the bastard horning in on my territory. *Christ.* I have to stop thinking like that. I'm not a dog pissing on what's his, and Keelie Sue isn't a goddamned tree. She's a person.

"He's gonna bring your car by your place," I say, because I figure she'll want some kind of explanation, and Fang needs the instructions. Not that anyone in his right mind would steal her junker car, but she's probably attached to it. Girls name crap and get sentimental.

I feel her nod and watch her fingers tug free from Fang's grasp. A second later, she slides her arms back around me and holds on like she kind of wants to burrow inside me. She doesn't like Fang, and I have to agree with here there. If I take over the pack, he's the first to go.

I pull out of the parking lot and take us onto the street. There isn't much to see in this part of Baton Rouge. The scenery is mostly warehouses, empty lots, and the occasional wino or druggie. A few semis park on the street while the drivers crash or unload, and grass grows through the sidewalk in spots. It isn't the kind of place you vacation, and it damned sure isn't the bayou.

I've never been a city boy. I love the bayou, love running as a wolf through the swamp. No matter what happens, I won't give that up.

Keelie Sue doesn't ask questions, but she does hold on. Living with Big Red has clearly done a number on her head because the women in my pack would kick me in the balls if I tried dragging them around like my own personal piece of meat. I suck in a breath of air as we pick up speed, and try to sort out my thoughts. Since when has Keelie Sue become *family*? I hardly know her, although I've seen her at more than one club function. Big Red likes his female accessories, and he often parks his daughter by his side. Usually she looks like she's trying to fade into the woodwork, and I've been able to overlook her.

*Liar.*

Okay. So what if I know exactly where she is and what she's doing? She's pretty. I have eyes in my head and a working dick. Just makes me not dead.

Breaking a few traffic laws, it takes less than ten minutes to get us to Belle Plantation, and then I kill the bike and coast to a stop. I kinda want to turn around, see what Keelie Sue thinks of my pack's place, but that's all kinds of wrong too. I shouldn't have taken Big Red up on his dare, shouldn't have brought her out here. Hell, *Cruz* is likely to take issue with my bringing her here.

"Hold this." I shove the key I fish out of my pocket into her hand, and she grasps it automatically. The driveway is gravel. Isn't like she can walk over that barefoot, so I swing her up in my arms and head for the door. She squeaks and stiffens in my arms. I'm getting kind of tired of that, frankly.

Jesus. If I put her down now, would she run? I'm not risking that, so I shuffle her around in my arms, pry the key out of her fingers, and get us inside and up the stairs without being spotted by any of my family. That's a miracle right there, but I'll take it. My room is kinda empty since I use it for sleeping and not much else. I have a four-poster bed that's some kind of antique from a gazillion years ago and a chair, but that's it. I should order some crap from a Pottery Barn catalog or something, but I haven't had time for interior decorating. Running with two packs takes a shitload of time.

My phone buzzes, and I'd lay money on it's being Cruz. In addition to being the Alpha of our pack, the sheriff of Port Leon, and my older brother—all of which guarantee he sticks his nose in my business and tells me how to manage my shit—he's practically omniscient. He's probably heard about my impromptu date with Keelie Sue and wants to know what the fuck. It's what I would ask in his position.

I look around for a place to stash Keelie Sue. Isn't like I have many choices. I have the bed... or the floor. Bed it is. I let her drop, she squeaks (naturally), and I turn away to take my call. Caller ID promises I'm about to have fun times with Cruz.

"You really wanna rip into me now?" I start with the easy questions.

The pause on the other end doesn't last long. "You really wan' to take over the Breed?" My brother sounds downright mellow. All that calm is an act. Cruz loves the rules, he loves our pack, and he loves me. Not that we talk about our feelings, but some things go without saying. My pulling a disappearing act with Keelie Sue breaks the rules and sets me up to be the new Alpha of the Breed. Can't be part of Cruz's pack if I have my own, so keeping her around puts me on a collision course with my brother, and neither of us wants that since the whole love-and-affection train runs both ways. Still, the Breed needs a reorganization in the worst way, and I can do it. Only question is whether I'll do it *well*.

"Not a question of wanting," I admit. I lean against the wall and watch my Friday night companion sit up. She doesn't bolt for the door, although that might have something to do with my own proximity to the exit. I'd be on her before she could get a hand on the knob.

Cruz curses. "Tell me this is just sex."

I eye Keelie Sue again. She's the prettiest thing I've ever seen, but she's more than a hot body. More than a free meal ticket and all-access pass to pack leadership too. It would be convenient if I could bang her and leave, but I don't see that happening. "Could be," I agree.

But it isn't. Stupidest idea I've ever had, but I don't

just want to grind my dick into every hole Keelie Sue has. That would be too simple.

"You screw with an Alpha's daughter, and he's either goin' to castrate you or promote you," Cruz growls. "You really wan' to fuck her that badly?"

Possibly. Unfortunately that's only the tip of my sexual iceberg. I want way more than sex, but I'm *not* telling my brother that wrapping an arm around a female and holding her close is on my to-do list. He doesn't need the ammunition. "Someone needs to do something about the Breed," I point out.

"Someone doesn't have to be you," Cruz tells me, sounding more tired than pissed off now. "I'm workin' on it. You know that. That's why you're *in* the fuckin' club in the first place. You're my wolf."

Keelie Sue shifts on the mattress, drawing her knees up to her chest and wrapping her arms around them. She puts her head down and her breath shudders out of her in a little sigh. Or maybe it's a fucking sob, because apparently, I scare her half to death. What she hasn't figured out is that I'm not Cruz's wolf anymore—I'm *hers*.

## KEELIE SUE

I can't make out too much of his brother's side of the conversation, but several things are perfectly clear. First of all, Cruz Jones already knows what happened tonight. He knows that my dad offered to mate me to his future replacement. Since Cruz also knows that I'm here with Jace—wherever *here* is—he has to believe that Jace is seriously considering the offer. And that explains the extreme displeasure in his voice.

Through the curtain of my hair, I watch Jace shake his head. "I'm not your wolf," he says finally, sounding impatient and terse, and nothing like the wolf who offered to spank me until we both enjoyed it. Oh. God. I need to not think about playing kinky sex games with Jace, but I can't douse the heated arousal that unfurls in my body.

Jace isn't mine. If he isn't Cruz's, then to whom *does* he belong? If my dad wins, I lose. The only reason I can imagine Jace walking away from his family is if he decides to start his own pack… or if he acquires a ready-made pack. The Breed wolves are nothing like the Jones wolves, or so I've heard. That doesn't mean that I want Jace to play a starring role in my personal life—even if my sex life is open to debate. Plus, I have no proof that Jace is interested in anything more than a fast pass to Alphadom.

I've heard that there are packs that believe in fated mates. Once upon a time that sounded kind of romantic to me—guy sees you and falls madly in love because you're the most beautiful goddess he's ever seen? That's fantasy fodder right there. Then I realized that Mr. Wolf couldn't possibly know much more about his bride than her cup size and the color of her hair. As a basis for long-term happiness—or even a less awkward morning-after—it sucked.

Jace ends the call and jams the phone back into his pocket. My reprieve is over. I run through my options as he strides back to the bed and stands over me. I can lie back, hope that he won't hurt me too badly, and let Big Red mate us like bunnies. Jace is probably banking on my going with that option.

Alternatively, I can make a break for it. I won't get far. He'll bring me down, and then we'll be back to the having-sex-because-I-have-to option. Option three… kill the man. Somehow. I'm no MacGyver to take down a man with my bare hands. None of my options are working for me.

He drops onto the bed and plants a knee beside me. The mattress dips and I scramble away. It isn't dignified, although Jace pretty much killed my dignity for the night after he hauled me out of the club over his shoulder, flashing the world my undies.

"Shit," he announces roughly.

We're in total agreement there. That one word sums up my current situation. He snags my wrist and tugs carefully, pulling me back into the center of the bed. He's too close, too big, too... male. My brain broadcasts a *run, bitch!* message on a loop, but then my wolf surprises me. My wolf actually thinks pressing closer is the best idea we've had all night. He can protect me, and the sex might even be awesome. He might be rough and more than a little rude, but I like everything else about my biker wolf.

"You think I asked for this?" I blurt out the words, then bite my lip. Probably should go for something sexy, something that might convince the man to bend to my will in this one little thing.

"Nope," he agrees, much to my shock. "You think I'm that hard up that I need my girl to be forced to be with me? I'm not into manhandling you or rape, got it?"

"Understood." Maybe he's the one with other, better options, because it's not like he's starved for sex. I've seen more than one club pass-around with her lips wrapped around Jace's dick. The wolves aren't shy, and sex is as common as beer, particularly in the shadowy corners of the club's base. I moved on quick because I'm not into porn shows, but I couldn't help but notice a few things. Like how his eyes never stopped examining his surroundings and how his hand stroked lightly over the girl's head. Kind of like she was a favorite pet, or maybe he was a little bit bored. If that had been my mouth sucking him deep, I'd have *made* him pay attention to me. Lips, tongue, or teeth—it would have been up to him.

Surprise number two? He lets go of my wrist. The other wolves would have been all over me by now. He nudges my chin up so he can look me in the eyes.

"I mate you, I get the pack."

"Sounds like it," I agree. I don't have to like the truth.

Then Jace surprises me. "How do you feel about it?"

I freeze because that has to be a trick question. Or code for *remove your clothes and let's make our family merger a reality.* The pack leaders don't ask for my opinion—and it isn't an oversight on their part. My dad doesn't want to know how I feel, and he damned certain doesn't place any kind of value on my insights or opinions. I'm a tool, a commodity.

"If you need to think on it, I've got all night," he says, amusement filling his voice. I don't think he's laughing at me, but I also don't know what the joke is. He rolls onto the mattress and stretches out his legs. The man certainly fills out a pair of blue jeans.

"I don't want another mating," I admit.

"First one didn't go so well," he agrees and his words aren't a question.

*Not so well* is an understatement.

"You need to talk about it?" He sounds pained, and I bite back a snort of laughter that is as unexpected as it is welcome. My dad practically gift wrapped me and threw me at Jace—and Jace carted me off caveman style. Now he's offering to be…

"You want to be girlfriends now?"

"Not really," he says, and it's kind of cute the way his voice gets all growly when he's embarrassed. "But if you've gotta get things out, I can figure out how to listen."

My Alpha gave me an order. I look over at him cautiously. He seems relaxed, his hands stacked under his head. No matter how big the mattress is, though, I can't avoid bumping into him, and each casual touch sends another lick of heat through my stupid, traitorous body.

"There's nothing I want to say about Bolt."

There was plenty of speculation about how, exactly, my first mate died. My dad paired us together, and we went off into the bayou for "a romantic honeymoon." Which was bullshit, pure and simple, but I'd been far too young to run. So I went. I got on Bolt's boat, and I let him take me out to his hunting cabin. He did things to me, and I survived. He then proceeded to drink too much Jack Daniels, and when he got back into the boat... there's a reason why everyone warns against drinking and driving. I didn't have to do a thing. I stood on the dock and watched him drive into a cypress, and then I stood and watched while the gators finished him off. I'd have pushed him in, but I hadn't had to. Mother Nature and his own stupidity had taken care of everything for me.

"Okay," he agrees, to my surprise. "We don't gotta talk about him."

"Thank you," I say, and he snorts.

"You don't have to thank me for that." He rolls closer as he says it, and I can't hold back a flinch. He's so big, and we're absolutely, totally alone. Whatever he decides, I can't stop him.

He freezes. "Fuck."

Now, see? That's exactly what I'm worried about. I slide backward on the mattress a few more inches. Pretty soon, I'll be on the floor. His hand finds my hip, anchoring me when I teeter on the edge.

"Have I ever hurt you?" Jace sounds annoyed now, but not angry. So things could be worse. I saw him tear into a prospect once. The kid had done something Jace hadn't liked, but my takeaway had been that I couldn't survive that kind of anger.

The coiled tension in the large body next to mine is unmistakable, but I have no idea how to fix the situation. Since the room and the bed don't provide many hiding places, I settle for a shrug. There's nothing I can say anyhow—or at least nothing that he wants to hear.

"Your daddy's gonna ask if I touched you," he whispers roughly. He unzips my borrowed jacket and then his thumb rubs a slow, heated circle over my hipbone. To my surprise, some of my panic subsides. The rhythm is comforting, different from the pattern I would set, but not bad. Is it an accident, or did he notice that much about me?

"You're touching me now," I point out. "So you can say *yes* with a clear conscience."

"You bet," he drawls. His thumb doesn't stop its slow, hypnotic glide, dipping beneath the sweatpants to find my bare skin and the lacy band of my thong.

"So this is all for show?"

He gives me a wicked grin. "Nope. This part's for me and you, sweetheart. But you need to answer a question for me."

I stare at him, waiting. He'll ask. I'll answer. I just have no idea whether it will be enough, whether it will be what he wants. *What about what you want?* I shut the little voice down. What I want is to leave this room behind me, and then leave my pack. Right now the man holding me so lightly is my ticket to both events.

"Am I hurting you?" There's no missing the thread of amusement in his voice.

There are all sorts of *hurt*, but I go with the literal interpretation. Figure that's what he wants to hear anyway. "I'm fine," I tell him and he nods.

"I wanna kiss you now," he rasps. He moves and my back hits the mattress. I've never liked feeling trapped, and he presses me down, his body controlling

45

mine. He rests his hands on either side of my head, his fingers tangling in my hair, wrapping the strands around his wrist.

Kissing isn't my thing. It's way too personal. I don't need to know which brand of toothpaste he does—or doesn't—use. But he isn't asking. He's telling.

"Why are you really doing this?" I whisper.

"Because I want to," he tells me, giving me more of his weight. I can breathe. Barely. I can also feel the heat and the strength of him through my thin tank top, my nipples hardening against the lace of my bra. I don't know whether I'm more scared—or turned on. "And because you're so goddamned gorgeous, I could just eat you up."

I'm not beautiful, but the look in his eyes is heated. He isn't just giving me the words—he means them. Having a wolf shifter describe me as edible—when he has his mouth inches from my throat—should scare me half to death. And I don't feel entirely comfortable.

I give his chest a little push. "What if I don't want to?"

"I could convince you."

He settles his penis against my stomach. He's hard, and if I need more proof that he believes his own speech, I have it. Unexpected heat rushes through me, a new, surprising throb bursting into life between my legs. I might not like fucking shifters, but Jace Jones is the sexiest man I've ever seen and he's *inches* away.

"Let me," he teases roughly, his breath brushing my cheek, my mouth. If I struggle, maybe he'll let me go. Or maybe not. He's a wolf and a predator, and he has me pinned beneath him. The wolf won't hesitate to take what it wants—the pack survives because of its ruthless instincts. I don't know if Jace is more wolf than man or the other way around, but part of me doesn't care.

The part of me that is a living, beating heartbeat

between my legs. Stupid, reckless, *intoxicating* pleasure shoots through me.

"You can try," I say, knowing that no one dares Jace.

He grins slowly, and then that wicked, wicked mouth of his covers mine and he kisses me. I expected hard, his tongue invading my mouth. I expected him to take—instead he gives and suddenly I know exactly why all the women at the club seek him out. He kisses me slow and deep, his tongue licking over my lips, coaxing me to open up like it was my very own idea and a good one at that.

I open with a sigh, and he slips inside my mouth. He explores every inch of me, his tongue learning me in a sensual game of hide and seek. I hide. He seeks. And when he catches my tongue with his, I moan. Surrender feels so good. I kiss him and kiss him, curling my fingers into his shirt to drag him closer.

All the way closer. Jace Jones has me spread on a mattress beneath him, his penis pressed against me, and all I want is *more*. More of the heat burning through my body, more kisses. He's dangerous, and I forgot that because he's so very good at touching me.

Stupid. I force myself to remember what's at stake. I want out of the pack. I want to decide for myself what I'll do, where I'll go—and who I'll fuck. Jace threatens all of that with one kiss. When I pull back, he lets go of my mouth, but holds on to the rest of me. I push back into the mattress, but where can I go? His arms cage me in place, his legs hold me down. And I like it far too much.

I've never liked anything so much, which means I need to get away.

"This isn't a good idea," I breathe. "I don't want a mate."

He rests his forehead against mine, his breathing rough. I'm not the only one who got lost in our kiss. "It's just a kiss."

47

Nothing is that simple in the pack. I shake my head.

"We both know that's not true."

His mouth brushing against my hair is unexpected. "You got a plan to leave?"

I shrug, willing him to let it go. "I'll figure something out."

He shakes his head, because he's clearly calculated my chances of walking away from Big Red and the Breed, and come up with the correct answer. Zero. Zilch. *Nada*. I was born a wolf, and I'll die a wolf. I just am hoping to postpone the dying day at least a few decades.

"You think about it. Think about taking me as your mate."

Truth is, mating isn't my choice, any more than those girls that Big Red has collected have a choice. He'll trot them out at the party, and his wolves will take their pick. And part of me, the part that's part lonely and all crazy, *likes* the idea of taking Jace.

My dad threw me at him, and he chased me and kissed me… but the one thing he hasn't done is hurt me. And that makes him the exception in my world.

"Go to sleep, sweetheart," he says roughly, his voice rumbling out of the darkness above my head. He's close enough that his words seem to brush my hair. My cheek. Close enough that I feel each small exhalation. Jace doesn't talk much, but he makes his words count.

"You in the business of telling me what to do now?" Asking questions is stupid when the man I'm asking has me trapped, but I feel like I'm finally waking up. Kind of like when you fall asleep in the afternoon and one minute the room is full of light, and the next it swims in later afternoon sunshine, shadows teasing the corners and your sleep-fogged eyes.

"I'm Alpha," he says finally, those two words a

statement of fact—and a promise.

"But you're not *my* Alpha," I counter. *Not yet.* I pluck the edge of the bed with my fingers.

"I will be," he tells me, and I don't doubt him.

I can imagine him as Alpha all too easily. My wolf already recognizes the strength in him and the easy way he dominates me. And as Alpha, he'd give me orders. For my own good, or the good of the pack, but he'd take over when he thought it necessary. I'd be bound to him instead of to my dad, but a change in ownership isn't freedom. Not really.

He eases the jacket off me, then wraps an arm around my waist and pulls me back against his body. The heat and the strength of him feel like the exclamation points on his sentence, punctuation I can't ignore. The only way he gets to be Alpha is if he *takes* the position—over Big Red's dead body—or he takes me. My body is like a living property deed, and my free will doesn't come into it. In the end, he'll always be physically stronger than me.

"I want to leave the pack," I tell him and the darkness around me. After a lifetime of being a good little Beta wolf, I want something more. Something for me.

He doesn't say anything for a long moment. My words sink into the silence between us, a plea, a threat. He can make me his mate and take the pack that way, but I won't make it easy for him. I'm not his all-access magical pass to Alphadom. The silence spins out between us, filled with unasked and unanswered questions.

"I could make you want it," he says finally, and it doesn't matter what the *it* is. Sex, mating, life with him. He's all solid muscle and male determination, and if he sets himself to doing something, he'll do it. Jace doesn't quit, and he doesn't lose. Part of me melts, thrilled that I could be the battle he'll pick to fight. The rest of me isn't ready to give up my dream of freedom.

"You get off on making people do things?" He stills behind me, and I can't tell if I've pissed him off or not.

"Could be." His hand presses against my belly, his fingers stroking the band of my panties where the sweatpants dip down. "But maybe you like getting told what to do."

"I've had enough orders for a lifetime, thanks," I tell him.

He snorts. "In bed, sweetheart."

"I've been told what to do there plenty of times too." I can't stop the bitterness from leaking into my voice. And you know what? I don't want to, either. I'm tired of pretending that I just love it when my dad passes me around like a party favor. If Jace thinks I'm here voluntarily with him, he needs a wake-up call. *Except maybe you* would *have come with him*, that stupid little voice in my head whispers. *If he'd bothered to ask.*

Jace certainly does more telling than asking. Witness our current conversation.

"Wish I could kill him for you," he says slowly. "Don't know what Bolt did exactly, but you did the right thing."

"He was an asshole." Somehow my head finds its way back onto Jace's chest, and I feel some of the tension leak out of my body. He's warm and solid—and surprisingly nice. Okay, he has a mouth on him, but I think he actually means it. He'd have killed Bolt for what he did to me, and that's the nicest thing anyone has said to me in ages. Which is screwed up.

"A dead asshole." The amusement is back in Jace's voice. He runs his thumb down my cheek. "If you didn't enjoy what he did to you, he did it wrong. And he shouldn't have done it."

I look down at the hard arm clamped around my waist. The room is so dark now, I can't make out the tattoo I know is there. But I can smell Jace, and his scent is wild and male, surrounding me. Crowding me. He wants something from me too, and I need to remember that, even if he has volunteered to be my own personal hit man.

"You want me to tell you all about it?" Teasing him is stupid, but I can't resist.

"Christ. No." He mutters the words against my hair. "Bolt fucked up. I wouldn't. You take my orders in bed, and you're gonna learn that submitting can be sexy. My fingers in your pussy, my tongue and my mouth eating you up and giving you that orgasm you want. You're gonna love every minute of it, that's my promise."

His mouth finds my ear, nips gently, fiercely where Big Red hurt me. Oh, God. Maybe he's right about this too, because heat floods through me. Unwelcomed, unwanted, fabulous heat. He makes me desperate for more, and all he's done so far is *bite* me.

"Jace—" I have no idea what words should follow his name. He nips my ear a second time, and the sharp, demanding sting makes me wet. God, I'm stupid. He's offering sex, and I'll bet the words *gentle, tender,* and *romantic* aren't part of his repertoire. He'll be straight up dirty in bed, and in another lifetime I might welcome him with open arms.

He runs a hand down my spine, his palm resting on the curve of my butt. "Say yes."

It would be so easy to say the word, to give Jace what we both want. One word, three little letters that would change everything, but this isn't just sex. I mean, it isn't some kind of romantic proposal with a big-ass diamond ring and promises of happily-ever-after either, but it's more than a condom and an orgasm. And bottom line? I can't afford Jace's price tag. He wants more than sex too. He wants a werewolf mate, and he wants to take my dad's place as Alpha of my pack.

51

"No," I whisper, slowly, reluctantly, and he pulls his hand away.

He rubs his face against my throat, marking me. We might not be having sex, he might not be willing to force me, but I'll return to the pack tomorrow covered in his scent. There will be no question about who I spent the night with, and assumptions will be made.

"I can't give you the *Princess Bride* shit," he mutters roughly against my skin. "If that's what you're holding out for." I must make some small grunt of confusion because he continues. "I can't be all *as you wish* and back the fuck off because you need space. I won't worship you from afar, and I sure as hell am not going to be your beck-and-call boy. I'm wolf, and you're gonna be mine, sweetheart, just as soon as we come to terms."

"You'll take what you want."

"You can take too," he says, his voice low and full of promise. "You can take *me* too."

Problem is, his definition of *take* isn't the same as mine. He still expects me to be submissive, and I don't know if I can do that again.

"I won't be doing any *taking*," I tell him then roll away. "Because I'm leaving."

JACE

Keelie Sue's timing sucks. While I like her grit, now isn't a good time for her to be running around Baton Rouge on her own. No two ways about it—her daddy painted a target on her pussy. Right now, I'm the asshole who owns her, and I take that responsibility seriously.

"Not a good idea, sunshine."

While I don't need the dating help, and the whole lack-of-choice thing is far too dub-con for my tastes, facts are facts. If she leaves and another Breed wolf finds her, he'll take her rough and hard. She'll end up hurt and that's unacceptable. She deserves a better mate than me, but I'm the best option she has tonight.

No getting around that truth.

While I'd be happy to persuade my little wolf to get naked with me, I'd planned on doing that with kisses. Kiss her mouth, her throat, and if my luck held, her sweet, tight pussy. Bet she'd taste good on my tongue, me licking her folds and shoving my tongue inside her hot, wet hole. I'd make it good for her, make her want me—but that is all the *making* I'd do.

Rape isn't my thing, and we fought a war in this country to end slavery. If Keelie Sue was human, she'd either tell me to fuck off after Big Red pronounced her temporarily mine, or she'd strip down and hop into bed with me because it's what she wants to do anyway. I have a feeling she's a true submissive at heart, which means I actually have a chance of making her happy in bed.

"Lie down," I tell her. I spent most of the week riding on club business and then I took down a pack of wolves at the clubhouse. I'm fucking tired. If I get nothing else out of tonight, I'm getting some sleep.

In answer, she slides her legs over the side of the mattress. She has gorgeous legs, long and toned, and the itty-bitty leather skirt is exactly the kind of picture frame I love. For a long moment, I just enjoy my view.

"I'm not a submissive," she announces defiantly, shoving to her feet. She looks horrified—and embarrassed. Fuck. That wasn't my intention.

"Nothing wrong in taking orders." Hell, I plan to teach her all the sweet pleasures of submission. I want to put my cock inside her everywhere, and I have more than a few fantasies about fucking her in the ass.

53

I'd warm her up good, have her ride my fingers until she whimpered with pleasure, maybe spank her a few times for good measure. I'd make damned sure she enjoyed every second of her submission.

"You think I can't do this without someone telling me what to do?"

To be honest, I have no idea what *this* is. Don't really give a shit, either. It's cute the way she gets all upset, kind of like watching a kitten hiss and spit. Maybe I'll get her one. Bet she'd like that almost as much as I like the fact that her scent doesn't include a single note of fear anymore. I have her alone in a bedroom, and she's pissed off.

"Maybe you should clue me in, sweetheart." I curl my hand around her thigh, tugging her toward me. She slaps at my fingers and I grin.

"I can have sex. Any time at all," she announces, and I choke. Hadn't seen that one coming. At all.

"Didn't think you wanted to jump me," I drawl, loving the way her eyes flare. "But I'm all yours."

"I don't." She bites her lip, then shakes back her hair. "I do this all the time, and you're just not that interesting."

"Seen one penis, seen them all?"

I didn't expect her to make me smile.

She smooths a hand down her skirt. The too-short strip of fabric stops a mere three inches south of her butt.

"Uh-huh." I pat the bed beside me. "Come over here and lie down. We're going to go to sleep. You can work out our sex life tomorrow."

Being a gentleman sucks.

"You don't want me?" The look she gives me makes me want to do something. Don't know if it's shove my tongue in her mouth and play show-and-tell—because I'd be all over her in a heartbeat if that was what she really needed right now—or to pull her close. If she's turned me into a cuddler, I'll never live it down. But fuck me, it isn't a question of wanting. It's a question of what's right—and of taking care of her. If we have sex right now, she won't enjoy it, and then I'll have to kick my own ass.

"Are you forgetting who's the Alpha here?" I pat the bed again.

She doesn't move, and I kinda like the show of spirit. Nice to know pack life hasn't ground her down completely. "I know who's the asshole. I'm going back to my own place. Alone."

"Not a chance," I growl. She doesn't get to make stupid decisions that put her in danger. "You're the Beta. You submit. I'm the wolf who owns you tonight. If anyone's getting inside you tonight, I'm the man."

I crave her like a fucking drug, but she's tired too, and she's had a shit night. Her dad loaned her out like a spare bike, and that has to hurt. As her future Alpha, I have one job—to take care of her.

Even if that means ignoring the raging hard-on I'm currently sporting.

"I'd like to see you try." She actually turns and heads for the door. No fucking way. I'm off the bed in a flash, slapping a hand on the doorframe. I don't hold it shut. No, I want her obedience, and I'll have it. She'll back down, we'll go to bed—and *not* have sex—and in the morning, I'll figure out how to convince her she wants to be my mate.

"Don't," I growl against her ear.

She stills. "Or what?"

"Or I'll spank your pretty ass."

"Try it," she snaps, sassy as hell, and then dances away.

"I take requests." I prowl closer. "If I have to spank you to keep you safe tonight, you've got it. It's your choice."

She looks over her shoulder at me, her hand reaching

for the knob.

"Stay," I bite out. She drives me crazy. I want to protect her, and yet she insists on marching straight out of my arms and into trouble. Because I have no doubts whatsoever that trouble will find her tonight, and that whatever form that trouble takes, she'll end up hurting.

That's unacceptable. I flatten my palm over her hand, covering her fingers with my own.

"You want me to stay? Convince me," she taunts, her eyes holding mine. For the first time in forever, she meets my gaze with her own and I have no idea what the fuck she sees in me. Every inch of her body screams a feminine challenge, and she's wolf. She *knows* what happens when a wolf challenges her Alpha.

"Last chance." I lean in, my weight pinning her in place, my mouth brushing against hers.

"You gonna spank me?" She breathes her question against my lips and those four, defiant words set me on fucking fire. She reaches behind her, tugging on the handle, and damned if she doesn't get the door open an inch. Guess I should have locked it. I fix that problem, then haul her over my shoulder and return to the bed. Keelie Sue has a lesson to learn. I'm not going to hurt her, but I'm in charge here and I'll keep her safe.

I strip her down. It doesn't take long. One good tug and her skirt flies across the room, and then I have her tank top over her head. She has on a real pretty red bra-and-panty set. Just the sight of her nipples threatening to bust through the lacy cups has me rock hard, and from the way her eyes widen, she notices.

I'm impressive like that.

Since I'm bigger and stronger too, it doesn't take much effort to wrestle her over my knee.

"Let's discuss who's in charge here," I growl.

## KEELIE SUE

Oh. My. God.

Where is my sense of self-preservation? Or self-respect?

Jace yanks me over his knee, his big palm smoothing over my panty-clad butt, and I actually don't want to kill him. It might have something to do with the way my new position jams my clit against his jean-covered knee, because when I wriggle, heat sparks through me. My inner hussy jumps up and down with glee, my wolf growling her agreement. *She* likes this game. *She'd* let Jace take charge because there's no way he'll let us leave without an orgasm. Or three.

"You got something to say to me, Keelie Sue?"

Some inner devil I didn't know I possessed makes me buck against his hold, and he brings his palm down on my butt in a short, sharp smack that stings more than it hurts. Delicious heat spreads through me, but not an ounce of outrage.

"I could do this all night," he bites out. "You got any idea how pretty your butt is, all pink from my hand? You're gonna think about me tomorrow when you sit."

He delivers another couple of sharp taps, each smack pushing my clit against his knee. I don't need to wait until tomorrow to think about him—he's front and center in my head right now. There's a sting in each slap, but it eases almost immediately into a delicious burn. Instead of hurting, his touch arouses me. I rise up to meet the next smack.

"You have a thing for kink, Keelie Sue?" He smooths his hand over my heated butt, soothing the burn and flooding me with pleasure. I wriggle, desperate for more contact. More *Jace*.

He notices too. He presses his knee up, and pleasure bursts through me. I'm supposed to stop him, to give him the words he demands and admit he's my Alpha, but then *he'll* stop.

And I love the way he makes me feel. I'm hot and needy, but he'll take care of me. He'll make sure I get my orgasm at the end.

"I think you like this," he rasps. "You like my being in charge, my making sure you come. Is that it?"

Jace is pushing. He wants me to back down and so he's trying to shock me, but it's like his touch flips some previously unknown switch inside me. He pisses me off, he scares me… and he turns me on. I only have one word for him now.

"Yes," I moan, pushing against his leg. He rewards me with another tap on my butt. *So good*. Funny how he's my big, bad, dangerous wolf and yet I feel safe when he puts his hands on me. That's a first for me.

"Maybe I should make sure you stay put."

Before I realize what he intends, he lashes my hands to the bed posts. I want the orgasm he's almost given me spanking me even more than I want to know what comes next. The thought of being at Jace's mercy makes me wet—because he won't show any. Truth is, it's so easy to let him take charge, to give me pleasure. The spanking and the ropes? They're just a way to make it even easier.

And since I liked it, I don't protest too much about my new bonds. Untied, I'd feel like I should run away, or like I should be doing something. Kissing him or making him feel good—doing something to bring about my own orgasm. This way—*his* way—all I have to do is lie back and enjoy it. He's made the touching all about me, and that's another first for me.

He slides down my body with a groan. "Last chance."

"For what?" When did my voice get so breathy?

"Before the big, bad wolf eats you up." He speaks the words roughly, as if he's daring me to do something, but I feel each small puff of air right *there* on the center of my panties, where I'm wet and swollen. No way I stop him now when I'm so close.

"Okay," I whisper and he strokes a thumb down my core.

"Say it louder," he demands.

"Finish me," I say out loud. "Do it right."

My butt stings, and I'm so wet I melt for him. Surely he won't make me wait any longer? And he doesn't. Thank God, he doesn't. He tugs and my panties rip or fly off or miraculously disappear—I don't care—and I'm bare and he's spread me open with his thumbs. I suck in a breath, and then he covers me with his mouth and it's all I can do not to scream.

He licks me from my bottom to my top, dragging his tongue through my cream with a hoarse sound of pleasure. I might be the one who's tied up, but suddenly I have all the power. I spread my legs wider, rocking into his tongue.

There isn't an inch of space between his mouth and my pussy. For just a moment I worry. About what I look like, smell like, taste like... and then he does exactly as he promised. He eats me up, and each lick, each taste drives me higher and higher, until I'm lost in the heated sensations.

He tongues me, and I hear myself cry out as I grip his head with my thighs, trying to drag him closer still. I'm so slick I can hear my wet as he traces a particularly wicked path around my clit and then he nips, and that last sting sends me over the edge.

It's embarrassing and fantastic and the most intense orgasm of my life. I come rubbing my pussy against his face, shrieking his name, and right then he owns me and we both know it.

## JACE

I intended to teach Keelie Sue a lesson. Instead, she schools me. She comes yelling my name, and I'm hers. She bargained for an orgasm, and got a mate.

Don't have an excuse for what I do next, either. As she pants and mewls her way through her orgasm, I rip open my jeans, whip out my dick, and pull back. With one hand, I cup her and pet her down from her high, her slick, wet pussy milking my hand. I slap my other hand around my dick. Two hard strokes and I finish too, my come covering her boobs, that pretty red bra, and her belly. My wolf growls a protest—*he* wants to fill her up, mark her from the inside out, and leave her with a baby in her belly.

Jesus. I didn't intend to go this far.

I'm not even inside her, and it's the best fucking orgasm of my life. My come marks her skin and I kind of want to beat my chest and roar. Fuck me, but she gets to me. She was supposed to call my bluff. Say *stop*. Instead she fucking asked for more—and instead of giving it to her slow and sweet, convincing her to take a chance on me, I went at her rough and hard.

I have no right to do that.

Even if I enjoy the hell out of it. The ropes are partly to make a point about what happens to naughty girls who try to break the rules, and partly because it's fun. I run a finger down the sweet curve of her throat, tracing the soft skin of her chest. Her breath catches, then goes ragged. The sweet scent of her arousal teases me. She came screaming my name—and that's a good thing—but now that I've accomplished what I set out to do, I'm not liking myself much.

I didn't spank her hard. I was making a point, not trying to hurt her. If she plays games with me, I'll win, and she needs to understand that. I'm Alpha to her Beta, and another wolf would hurt her bad to establish his dominance. Pleasure works even better, and we've both enjoyed the lesson.

Her nipple hardens as I watch. I stretched her out good, an arm and a leg bound to each bedpost. Not tight enough to hurt, but enough that we'll find out if she has a thing for kink. Kinda want to take a picture too, because I want to remember tonight, and that only makes me the frontrunner for bastard of the year. Doesn't take too much effort to imagine her reaction to photographic evidence of tonight's fan-fucking-tastic sex.

"Now would be a good time to get started on that apology," I tell her. At the very least, I should untie her. Even though keeping her safe is my top priority—*always*—keeping her here will get complicated, fast, because it will be seen as my making a bid to take over the Breed, and I'm not ready to seal that deal yet.

She sucks in a breath, shifting on the bed like she needs to get closer to me. I lean in. Maybe I'll kiss her. Find out for myself what she thinks about the two of us. Christ, she smells good, like vanilla and woman.

The hard rap on the door sends her scrambling backward.

Not like I really need a wake-up call, but seems I get one anyway. The scent at the door belongs to Cruz, and if my brother's knocking when I'm holed up with a female, things aren't looking up.

"Fuck off," I yell, knowing words aren't going to cut it. Isn't like there's a no-females rule, but the pack sticks to the shadows, lurking in plain sight of the human world. We don't invite their attention, and my bringing Keelie Sue here is a big fucking red flag. Plus our *maman* won't like it either. Not if it looks like I have to tie Keelie Sue up to keep her. Our *maman* won't tolerate a forced mating—or even the semblance of one.

I'm stupid as fuck.

"You got to the count of three," Cruz announces. He sounds pleasant, like he's just stopped by to chat me up about the weather or to offer me a beer. Knowing Cruz, that means he's about to lose his shit big time.

I jackknife off the bed with a curse, buttoning up my jeans. When I crack the door, Cruz shoves it open further. He takes in my room and the bondage scene, his face not giving away anything. I'm shirtless, but I've kept my jeans on and my boots. Still, I'm closer to naked than I need to be, and the scents Keelie Sue gives off aren't helping, either. She smells of arousal and curiosity. A man would have to be dead to not take her up on that luscious invitation.

"Introduce me," Cruz growls. He knows exactly who I have with me, so his words are intended to make a point.

I move farther into the doorway, blocking his view of my female.

"You angling for an invitation to join us?"

Keelie Sue makes another one of those cute, tiny noises and tries to crawl into herself. She's not into that particular kind of wolf party—that much is clear.

"Fuck you," Cruz tells me, and I'll pass on that. Since he's waiting for an explanation, however, I pony up a few words. Maybe then he'll go away and leave Keelie Sue and I alone to sort out whatever it is that's happening between us.

"I'm rescuing her," I tell Cruz when he raises a brow.

*From herself*, I add mentally. After all, she can't go running around Baton Rouge with half of Big Red's pack looking for her.

"That doesn't look like any *rescue* I've seen." But

Cruz studies my face, avoiding the scene inside the bedroom. Since Keelie Sue doesn't want him looking, he's playing the gentleman.

"The boys down at the motorcycle club gave her to me." Big Red's callousness pisses me off all over again. Keelie Sue is special, and her father should know that. Should be protecting her from wolves like me. Bottom line? I won't hurt her.

Ever.

Okay, won't hurt her *much*. I bet her pussy is tight as shit, and she'll be sore the day after I have her. I promise to kiss it better though, and some things hurt good.

Cruz doesn't budge from the door. "You'd better be getting a clear *yes* from her before you go anywhere near that bed."

The urge to hit my brother is almost overwhelming. Cruz knows me better than that. He *knows* I won't go where I'm not invited. We're playing a game, Keelie Sue and I, a complicated, fucked-up, sexy-as-hell game. Keelie Sue is a Beta wolf, unlike Cruz's woman. Gianna would kick his balls into the middle of his throat if he pulled this kind of shit on her without permission, but Keelie Sue is different. She'll push back if she has to, but her wolf also trusts me to look out for her because I'm going to be her Alpha.

It's that fucking simple.

Of course, if I were a decent Alpha, I'd pat her on the head, take her back to her place, and let her go. I'm not like Cruz, however, and I can't do that. The urge to hang on to Keelie Sue, to mark her, to *keep* her is overwhelming.

So I settle for telling Cruz part of the truth. "If I claim her as my mate, I become the Breed Alpha." When he gives me a pissed-off look, I continue. "You should see the other candidates. I'm her best option."

At least I won't hurt her—or that's what I'm telling

myself. She can come after me all she needs, and I'll never hurt her back.

"So you all told her she had to pick wolf A, B or C? You boys never heard of *D: None of the above?*"

Cruz knows how a pack works. "They'd eat her alive."

"We're gonna talk about this more," he warns me. "You don' get to add kidnappin' to your shit list for this week. Our pack doesn't need that kind of trouble. Not now."

I cross my arms over my chest. "She's not gettin' hurt anymore."

Keelie Sue hasn't had a good day, but I planned on taking good care of her tonight, right up until the moment when she challenged me. Then okay, my plans got sidetracked and I tied her up, but I'm still optimistic. I inhale, not sure how to convey all this to Cruz or if it's any of his business at all—because I'm closer and closer to leaving our pack and taking one of my own and we both know it—when I scent a new wolf. We have an outsider running on our land.

"Pack business," I growl, dropping a kiss on her mouth. I have to go. Cruz needs me at his back. I hate leaving Keelie Sue, but duty calls. I cover her up with a blanket, ignoring the way her mouth shapes the word *fucker*. She isn't wrong.

## KEELIE SUE

At some point, I fall asleep. I dared Jace to spank me, knowing no Alpha wolf would resist a challenge. He did it, I loved it, and then I came howling his name.

Those things are equal parts embarrassing and good. I've never had an orgasm that intense, and he hasn't even come inside me.

The part where he leaves me, however, sucks. Worse, he leaves me tied up. Pack business bangs on the door, and he doesn't so much as acknowledge me. Two words and one hard kiss on the mouth doesn't count, not in my book.

So fuck him.

I'll get myself untied, I'll get up, and I'll go... away. Unfortunately my Girl Scout skills are rusty, and getting my hands free proves impossible. I'm also boneless from Jace's kisses, and sleep proves as irresistible as that damned wolf. Somewhere between midnight and dark o'clock, I fall asleep. I wake up with the damned wolf between my legs again.

Jace has untied me and flipped me over. It takes me far too long in the darkened room to figure out what's happening, or maybe that's because he has his mouth on my pussy, his tongue licking and sucking.

Oh. God.

"Jace?" I ask just to drive him a little mad. It's only fair.

"You expecting another wolf?" He punctuates his words with the wickedest thrust of his tongue into my channel. "I promised to kiss everything better after I spanked you. I always keep my promises."

He doesn't seem to want an answer, so I spread my legs a little wider, and he rewards me with another long, slow lick. When I moan, he does it again. And then again. He smells like the outdoors, like something wild and free, and yet I hold him there between my legs and he makes me feel like the most special thing in the world. He just keeps loving me with his mouth until I melt for him, and then he carefully moves up my body and pushes deep inside me. Over and over again he thrusts, filling me and holding me tight. I dig my nails into his broad, bare shoulders, tucking my heels against the small of his back as I rise up to meet each powerful thrust. The orgasm is almost a surprise when it hits, the pleasure rolling through my body.

"All better?" I feel the words against my skin and in every inch of my body.

"The best." I rock against him and he comes with me, emptying himself deep inside me, and I hold him tighter. Afterward, he doesn't say anything, just wraps himself around me so that there's no way I could get off the bed and away from him. I'm here until he gives me permission to leave, but I also feel... safe. He promised he wouldn't be the wolf to hurt me, and he hasn't forced himself on me. He's no Bolt, that's for sure, which has to be the only reason why I fall asleep in his arms.

4

## KEELIE SUE

S OMEONE OFFERS YOU A girl and you take her?"
The deep voice drifts into the room. A wolf's voice,
low and raspy. The words themselves sound rough
around the edges, the way the males do when they've
spent more time shifted than not. He doesn't smell
like pack, although his scent holds a note of familiarity.

I roll over, bury my face in the mattress, and freeze.
I'm not tied up anymore. Adrenaline pricks me, followed by the need to run. To get the hell out of this
bed, this place, this life. The wolf outside is a wake-up
call I shouldn't ignore.

"I said *thank you*," Jace drawls. Boots hit the stairs
with a hard thump, the sound receding as they move
away. More distant, less distinct sounds follow as the
two men wrestle. Or possibly try to kill each other.
Fists thud on bodies, the sounds of combat punctuated
by the occasional harsh curse—or laugh. Neither man's

scent seems hostile, but I can't be entirely sure they aren't beating the crap out of each other. Maybe this is my opportunity to slip away.

I tried to remember the route to Jace's place last night, but it was late, I was scared, and he drove fast. I could probably do it, I decide. The problem is that I need wheels—which means either getting my hands on his keys, or waiting for him to take me back. I'm tired of waiting, so I slide off the bed quietly, and stand up.

Early morning light floods the room. Other than the stunning lack of furniture, Jace's place is gorgeous. The bed is set in front of a fireplace covered with white plaster roses and vines. The room also has honey-colored wood floors and floor-to-ceiling windows. I can see the green of the bayou through the gauze curtains.

A door leads out to what looks like a hallway and a staircase spirals down to the first floor. I dress rapidly—being naked is always a disadvantage when you're around wolves—and then ease my way toward the hallway and down the staircase. Ignoring the passageway that leads back into the house, I turn toward the front door. The *open* front door. Jace and the other wolf break apart before I cover half the distance. I press against the wall and inch closer.

I spot Jace's leather jacket dropped on the top step next to a coffee cup holder and a paper bag. Jace himself straddles a bronzed, dark-eyed wolf that grins up at him. The new wolf is scruffy, a bruise decorating the rough line of his jaw.

He turns his head and looks right at me. "You can come out, *boo*."

Jace curses and shoves to his feet, sliding his body between me and the other wolf. Since I hadn't precisely packed an overnight bag, I'm still wearing his sweatpants and my tank top. I'm barefoot and probably have a massive case of bedhead too. Sexy? Not so much.

Not that I want Jace to find me irresistible, but I have my pride—and there's that inconvenient attraction between us.

I eye the front yard, but Jace's place is clearly isolated. I see trees, trees, and more trees—plus a long, winding driveway and a gorgeous view of the bayou. Other signs of civilization? Not so much. A battered truck stands in the gravel driveway where he parked his bike the night before, but neither vehicle is any good to me without the keys.

"I'm Eli." The other wolf doesn't move from his prone position on the porch. He doesn't smile either, his face inscrutable. The laughter he shared with Jace vanishes as he examines me. I'm pretty sure he just found me lacking.

"She's trouble," Jace says, his words cutting through me. *See? He didn't mean he wanted to love you forever when he suggested you think about mating him for real last night.* He tosses me a saddlebag. "Eli stopped by your place and grabbed some things."

Maybe later I'll be creeped out by Eli and Jace's lack of boundaries, but right now I'm just grateful for clean underwear and a toothbrush that isn't pre-owned.

"Thanks?" *Please, please leave.* No, wait. I'm the one who wants to leave.

"You're a popular girl," Eli announces, rolling to his feet. I have no idea how to take that. Is he referring to last night's contest? To my dad's attempts to pair me off? Or has something else happened, and it's so horrible that even this wolf knows about it? Frankly, all three are possibilities.

Jace nudges the coffee holder toward me with his boot. "Breakfast of champions."

I'm not too proud to turn down coffee. I park my butt on the top step of the porch and grab a cup. There are pastries in the paper bag too, still hot from

69

the bakery. My opinion of Jace shoots up. Sue me. I'm weak like that. While I chew, Jace brings Eli up to speed on what happened last night at the Breed's clubhouse. Dad's wolves aren't supposed to discuss club business outside of the club, but either Jace doesn't give a fuck about the rules (which would come as no surprise) or he makes an exception for family. At least he stops at the part where we get on his bike and ride here. I don't need my sex life—or lack thereof—shared in public. When they both look at me, there's nothing I can do to stop the blush from heating up my cheeks.

"Cute." Eli whistles. "I thought the Breed tended to break their toys, though."

I open my mouth, but what can I say? Part of me agrees wholeheartedly with his assessment, while the rest of me is pissed off that he looks at me and thinks *toy*. Jace tugs me up onto his lap. My coffee cup flies, Eli catching it with casual power before it can spill. I've never figured out how any girl sits on a man's lap and makes it look good. Sure, it happens in the movies, but those are scripted scenarios. Jace's knees poke me in awkward places, and I'm embarrassingly aware of the heat of his thighs searing me through my borrowed sweatpants. He's no chair to relax into, that's for certain.

"Relax," Jace whispers against my ear. "Not gonna let you fall."

Falling is the least of my worries.

Then to Eli, he says, "Keelie Sue's stronger than she looks."

In all truth, there's only so much a woman can handle, and I've reached my maximum. Eli gives me an assessing look. "Wouldn't have thought it."

See? He agrees with me.

Jace laughs and snags my cup from Eli, setting it in my hand. "She's got her ways. Big Red's not gonna pass her around."

The vote of confidence is a nice surprise, but Jace is wrong. My dad absolutely would. Thinking about all the horrible things my father would do isn't productive, so instead I say what's been on my mind since last night.

"Fang said there were more."

Both wolves look at me. Their combined interest is more than a little overwhelming. I trace the top of my coffee cup with my finger. Left, circle the tiny hole in the plastic lid, then right.

"For the mating ball," I say into the silence. "Human girls."

I swear Eli's eyes glow. "What the fuck's a mating ball?"

Since he's a Jones, I guess he wouldn't know. And Jace joined us too recently for there to have been a ball in his time.

"The Breed throws a big party once a year. They call it a ball to class it up, but it's pretty much an open-bar kegger out in the bayou. He brings in a bunch of girls, and the wolves pick the ones they want."

"It's an orgy?" I can't tell from Eli's face if he's for or against the idea.

"Except the guys don't have to give back the girls at the end of the night." The words tumble out of my mouth faster and faster, mirroring the pace of my finger on the cup lid.

"*They* being the wolves—or the girls?"

I shiver, remembering my own mating night. "The wolves. The girls don't get a say."

"That fucking sucks," Eli says casually and without hesitation, and I agree. *Sucks* doesn't even begin to cover it.

"Could you—" I need Jace to agree with me, but I'm not much of a sweet talker. Okay, honestly? I'm not much of a talker at all. There's zero reason for him to listen to me.

"Do something? Yeah. What did you have in mind?"

I blank. I kind of want him to throw on a cape and go do his Superman-to-the-rescue impression, but that's not the world's most feasible plan.

"I don't want the other girls hurt," I say carefully. "I want them safe."

Which meant getting them out of there as far as I was concerned.

"You want to stage a rescue mission?" This time Eli does smile at me, and funny how a smile makes him seem like more of a scary-ass bastard rather than less. The man could make a Viking look like a mama's boy.

"I'd appreciate it," I say quietly.

"I'll see what I can do," Jace tells me, and I'll have to live with that. He scoops me off his lap and sets me on my feet. "Eli and I have to take care of something, so I'll take you home. See you later tonight at the clubhouse if not before."

## JACE

The run back to Belle Plantation clears my head. Or that's what I tell myself. Eli and I shifted after I drove Keelie Sue back to her apartment. Letting her walk away from me doesn't sit well, but I can't keep her with me.

Wolves pack Belle Plantation by the time I return. I haven't stayed out here much in the past couple of weeks, not since I bought my own place. Maybe my wolf sensed that I was coming to this moment, when I pull away from my birth pack and start looking for something more. It hurts though, at the same time that it feels right. Guess that's the way life rolls, and I'll have to get used to it.

If the Breed was just a pack of violent, no-good werewolves, I don't think I'd be so interested. That pack certainly has more than its fair share of assholes, but there are good wolves there too. Wolves who can't or won't break away from their pack because our kind doesn't do so well running as loners, and so they stay and none of them are strong enough to challenge Big Red or to turn things around. I can change that. Even without Keelie Sue by my side, I can challenge and win. I may be a cocky bastard, but I can fight and I'm mean to the bone. Big Red will go down, and then I'll have a new pack and Belle Plantation will never welcome me in quite the same way again. When I visit, I'll be an Alpha in my own right, a threat and an ally.

I debate whether my cousins have ever thought about forming a new pack. They lounge about the living room in their wolf forms, looking content as fuck. Since those boys usually don't come out of the bayou, I have to wonder if their presence means something, or if it's just a coincidence. Could be I'm paranoid too, after spending so much time with the Breed, where every gesture, every growl is a move in the dominance game.

My cousins are easygoing bastards who don't want to jockey for dominance in the pack—they know their worth and take turns playing the dominant when they're alone: rough loners, trackers, and hunters. Of course none of us fits the business suit crowd, and no one pushes us around. That's how the Jones clan has survived so long.

Cruz strides toward me before I can even close the door behind me. He's shucked his sheriff's uniform so he's officially off the human clock and all ours. It's a mystery how he balances living in two worlds, but he does. Of course, he also manages to share a woman with the Alpha of the Breaux pack.

Sort of.

I get the feeling that the details of that arrangement are a work in progress. Still, he gets a smile on his face that reaches all the way to his eyes when he talks about Gianna. She picked him and Luc, and if he's okay with her choice, the rest of us have to be as well. No killing the Breauxs—we'll focus on the Breed instead.

Of course, I've thrown a monkey wrench in that plan and all because I can't keep my dick in my pants.

It's too bad because things are finally settling down after Cruz and Luc nearly came to blows over Gianna. And if Cruz picks a fight, the rest of us follow. We have his back, no questions asked. Since Luc's brothers feel the same loyalty toward their Alpha, it leaves things plenty unsettled in the bayou. Cruz looks happy and relaxed, although the longer he looks at me, the more that look fades. Maybe kisses can make everything better, although I stopped believing that before I'd turned five.

"How's mated life?" I ask, coming to a halt.

"Gianna's cooking tonight," Cruz says, a small, private smile teasing his mouth. "Not sure if I should hurry home or not. Think it's her first attempt at something other than a Lean Cuisine."

The plantation has a smaller house set out on the edge of the garden. Place probably belonged to the estate manager in a previous century, but Cruz made it his own. Like all of us, he needs his space sometimes. Hell, now that he has a mate who comes with a bonus Alpha male accessory, he probably needs a blast zone around his walls.

"You better get used to telling her what she wants

to hear," I tell him with a wink. "Now that she's got you pussy-whipped and all."

His smile grows. He definitely knows something is up. "Hear I might have company on that front," he says finally. "Come on out back and we'll talk."

At least he isn't treating me to a full pack hearing. Right now, whatever he has to say to me, he intends to say it as my brother. That works for me. I follow him down the hallway that leads to the back porch. It looks downright good for a place where werewolves routinely run. We don't always mind our claws, and the woodwork and floors are collateral damage.

Outside, the bayou comes alive in the way I love. A bird calls in a rising scale of notes, almost drowned out by the noise of the crickets, and there is more than enough light to see the cousins' boats tied up at our dock.

A gator roars somewhere close by, hunting his dinner. Makes me think of Keelie Sue for about the hundredth time since I left her. Big Red mated her to Bolt and they found pieces of that wolf in the swamp. The gators hadn't left more than a torso, and rumor claims Keelie Sue didn't cry so much as a tear about her loss.

I lean against the porch railing and wait for Cruz to get started. He stares out at the water for a minute before giving me his full attention. Knowing Cruz, he's used that handful of seconds to organize his thoughts and come up with a battle plan. Cruz doesn't waste time, and he's damned decisive.

"The Breed's been a pain in our ass for months now," he says. "They've been running weapons and drugs in Baton Rouge, and the methods they use to hold their territory aren't methods I like."

All true. I definitely don't like their methods or, fuck, the end game. Not that I care much about human laws, but the way the Breed runs their territory is wrong. Big Red rules through fear and intimidation, using his fists and his teeth to literally tear down anyone who disagrees with him. It's one thing to be strong and earn your wolves' respect—even if that means the occasional dominance fight or beatdown, each blow has a purpose. Big Red is indiscriminate with his fists, and he likes dishing out pain way too much for my taste.

"None of us like it," I say. "That's why I agreed to go undercover with them."

"Not much cover," he disagrees. "They know you're a Jones."

I shrug. That's a detail that doesn't matter so much. "But they think I could be convinced to jump ship, to pick their pack over ours."

Cruz crosses his arms over his chest and looks at me. "A week ago, I would have agreed with that assessment."

"And now?"

"And now I have to wonder if there's some truth to it."

"If you've got something to say to me, say it."

He shakes his head. "It's not that simple, Jace. Big Red won't give up power—not willingly. But he *is* willing to make you promises about what happens someday—and seal those promises with Keelie Sue. Tell me that's not the truth, and we're done here."

"It's true," I allow. "He's recruiting, and he's cast his eye in my direction."

I've always been solid for Cruz, always had his back. After he assumed leadership of our pack, I slid easily into a new role as his lieutenant and Beta. Cruz doesn't give us orders. That's not how the pack works. He simply picks a direction and then he leads us in it. I've never had a problem following before, but now here I am trying to decide if I'll break away. Carve out my own place in the world. Haven't thought much about that before because I respect the hell out of

Cruz. Pack first. That's his rule, and that's mine too.

Keelie Sue's beat-up face kind of dances its way into my head though, and suggests that maybe she's pack too.

"You're thinkin' about it," Cruz says. I can't quite figure out what the look in his eyes is trying to tell me. Words would be simpler, or we could roll around, trading punches like we did when we were younger. Can't really tell if he's sad or happy or just mocking me.

"Maybe I am," I acknowledge. "Breed's been a pain in our ass for too long now, and this is one way to fix it."

My self-serving conclusion has Cruz laughing. "So you'd be taking one for the team?"

Fuck him. "Something like that. That pack's no good run the way it is. They're terrorizing their part of Baton Rouge, and Big Red's an ambitious cocksucker. He wants to control it all. Guns and drugs aren't gonna be enough for him, and we don't want that kind of trouble anyhow. He's already gotten his wolves arrested. Sooner or later one of them shifts in custody, and then all of the packs have a problem."

Cruz nods slowly. "Not sure how the humans would react to finding out they've got shifters living in their midst. It would be a goddamn PR nightmare at best, and it's something I'd rather avoid. Safer for everybody that way."

I hear him. One of the few checks on Big Red's wolves is the unspoken rule that nobody shifts in public. We keep our furry side on the down low, and that means terrorizing the old-fashioned way, with guns and fists. If the Breed ran the streets as wolves, adding teeth and claws to the mix, the outcome for Baton Rouge would suck.

There's something else Cruz needs to know too. "Keelie Sue said Big Red's got a bunch of other human girls locked up somewhere. He's planning on bringing them out at their next bonfire and any wolf there can take a bite."

"Fuck." Cruz scrubs a hand over his face. "He's dragging humans in here anyhow."

"Looks that way." It goes without saying that neither of us is okay with Big Red's kidnapping and rape agenda. Cruz's mate won't like it either if and when she finds out about it. "I'm gonna see what I can do to spring them, but I may need help."

And if any of those girls sees the wolves shifting, if they know exactly who and what the Breed are... well then we have ourselves a whole new set of problems that I have no idea how to solve.

And then Cruz lays it out there. I knew it was coming, but the words still hit me like a punch in the gut. "You wan' to stick with me, or are you striking out on your own?"

"I don't know yet," I give my brother the truth. Fair's fair.

He curses, but doesn't look surprised. "You got to tell me. You can't go surprising me with this shit."

"You're *famille*." I don't want to lose him or my place here. Any fights we have, we keep them private, and in public we present a united front. I don't want to cut myself off from our *maman* and dad, either. I know I'll never lose them entirely, but coming back here could get complicated if I take the Breed pack and things get messy.

"Yeah," he says. "We are. I don't wan' to fight with you, no matter what happens."

"Me neither."

"But the Breed plays by a different set of rules," he continues. "They don't care who gets hurt in the course of doin' business. There's more to them than bikes and riding fast, Jace, and it could be like riding the bull at the rodeo. Gettin' on isn't all that difficult because you got the bull in the chute to start, and those three walls and a gate kind of keep the beast in place, but once the rodeo starts, all bets are off. Not all of the Breed wolves are goin' to welcome a change in management, and they're goin' to test you."

"I can handle the challengers." I've watched the other wolves in the pack fight, and Big Red is right to be worried about me. I'm the strongest fighter.

"So why not challenge Big Red directly?" Cruz crosses his arms over his chest. "Why fuck around with the man's daughter?"

I can't explain why Keelie Sue interests me so much.

But she does.

Christ, does she ever.

## KEELIE SUE

T WO DAYS AFTER JACE dropped me off at my apartment, I'm back to work. Hello, Monday. I earned a bachelor's degree in accounting largely through online classes, because my dad wasn't in favor of my living on campus. I had a wolfish escort for the few classes I took on the local campus, and once I finished, he put me to work managing the club's cash flow.

Probably makes me dirty by association, but he does a good job concealing where the money comes from and how he made it. What I know is which bills need paying—the unsexy stuff like property tax and the electric—and then I invest the leftover money after I finish payroll.

Honestly, I love the work. Numbers make sense to me. They have a pattern, a predictable rhyme and reason, and there aren't too many surprises. After I first saw *Shawshank Redemption*, pretty much not a day went by when I didn't wonder if I could do what Andy Dufresne did and divert my dad's dollars into my own private retirement fund. I certainly wouldn't have a problem with living in Mexico, particularly not if it meant I could live pack-free. If wishes were horses, I'd have enough horses to run my own Preakness.

When my phone rings, it isn't good news. Since I've programmed the ring tone for my dad to play the *Jaws* theme, looking at caller ID isn't necessary. He doesn't wait for me to answer either, just starts talking as soon as I tap the talk button.

He isn't interested in hearing excuses or a status update—he just informs me that he's expecting me out at the mating ball on Saturday night and that by Sunday morning I'll be Jace's mate.

That's my dad's plan at any rate.

Now with the clock ticking, I still don't have any big ideas of my own. Part of me thinks using Jace's big body for my own personal sexy times isn't a *bad* idea, but the rest of me knows better. I don't want to mate him.

If Jace mates me, he'll own me.

Then my dad adds insult to injury by telling me more about "the girls" that "he and the boys" picked up for the mating ball. While I might be the star attraction—albeit I'm more *free gift with purchase* when all of the wolves are really jonesing for the leadership role in the pack—I'm going to have plenty of company. He has six girls lined up, or so he claims. Worse, he's planning on making one of them my new stepmomma. That's a resounding *hell, no* on my part.

My instincts clamor for me to get in my car and drive until I run out of gas. Since my dad doesn't trust me with much cash, and my credit cards are pack-issued, hitting empty wouldn't be far in my future. And even if I had a flush checking account and un-limited gas, it couldn't possibly take me far enough. I ran once, and my dad came after me. If I pulled a repeat, he'd come after me—and this time he'd kill me. He'd already fired the warning shot on that one, and I had the scars to prove it. So instead of running, I think about alternatives and doomsday scenarios.

By the time I walk into my apartment, all I want is a date with a tub of Ben and Jerry's, kind of like a last meal where I don't have to worry about nutrition or calories. What I get instead is a werewolf. Jace sprawls on my cherry-red couch, boots hanging off the end. He's banished my throw pillows to a haphazard mountain on the floor, and my fingers itch to line them up again. He wears his usual uniform of faded blue jeans and those big shitkicker boots I like far too much. He's tossed his leather jacket over a chair, and he sure looks like he's been waiting a while. My pulse kicks up, not sure there's a good reason for him to be here.

"You got to get better locks," he announces by way of greeting. "I'll set you up tomorrow."

I don't want him anywhere near my locks.

"Why are you here?" I actually consider running for the door. I'm close, close enough to make it. Probably.

He tilts his head back to meet my gaze. The position should make him look stupid, what with him hanging half upside down on my couch. It should *not* make him look sexy or approachable. I get the strong feeling that he knows I want to run—and he'll be on me before I can reach the door. Shoot.

"I'm giving you the chance to get to know me," he says cheerfully, and I consider picking up one of the abandoned pillows and lobbing it at him. He doesn't want me—he wants a job promotion and I'm the "interview" he needs to nail.

"I know all I need to know," I tell him, meaning every word.

"Hit me." He shoves upright into a sitting position.

For a moment, I think he means literally—and I'm kind of in the mood to take him up on the offer—before I realize he's asking me to 4-1-1 him. Does he really expect me to regurgitate everything I know about him?

"Don't tempt me," I mutter, heading for the bathroom. I'm fostering a litter of abandoned kittens and, while they've reached the age where they can be alone for a few hours while I work at the club, they still need plenty of TLC. Fortunately, I arranged for a neighbor to check in on them the night of my dad's party.

I keep the kittens in a cardboard box lined with towels, but one of the little rascals has scaled the sides during my absence. It sits in the middle of the floor, staring up at me reproachfully with dark eyes. Apparently I'm supposed to have installed a kitty elevator so it can return to the box at will. All of the kittens start talking up a storm when the door opens, recognizing the arrival of dinner. The kittens are almost ready to re-home and I miss them already.

I scoop up my escapee and nuzzle his tiny head with my cheek. I've mentally named this one Houdini, Fleet, Ninja Kitten, and Where-the-Hell-Did-You-Go-Now over the course of our time together. Kitten doesn't like having his world limited to four cardboard walls and a bathroom ceiling, and I can't blame him. We're kindred spirits like that.

Boots thud down the hallway behind me. "Jesus. You realize you're a wolf, sweetheart?"

Every day that ends in *y*.

The kittens must recognize a predator too, because they start hissing and spitting. Houdini arches in my hands, and I tuck him against my heart.

"The big bad wolf's coming to huff and puff and blow our house down," I tell the kitten.

Jace steps into my bathroom, and the room gets two hundred percent smaller.

83

"I thought the big bad wolf ate up misbehaving piggies." He wraps a hand around my hip and tugs until my butt and his dick are in happy alignment. My breath catches as I process his words. He can't possibly mean...

"Am I the pig in this scenario?" I wriggle. I'm not bending over to return Houdini to his siblings because I can feel the hard ridge Jace sports behind the fly of his jeans. Does the man walk around permanently erect?

"I'd be happy to eat you," he growls softly. *Oh. Wow.*

He's... offering me oral right here, right now? Is he serious? Because my inner bad girl is all ready to jump up and down and scream *pick me!* Or just scream. His fingers tighten on my hip, and I hold my breath.

He turns me on. I don't know why I have this thing for this particular wolf, but I'm seconds away from begging Jace to do his worst—because it would undoubtedly be *my* best and would make me some new memories. My breath catches, my lungs refusing to exhale as my whole body locks down on the erotic possibilities of me, Jace, and the bathroom. In the shower, on the floor—hell, up against the wall. There's no question he'd do it all.

"Now you've got nothing to say?" Amusement colors his voice.

"I think I should plead the fifth," I say honestly. He's gorgeous, and I want him bad, but he's also more than a little overwhelming.

"Uh-huh." He reaches around me, rubbing a finger over Houdini's forehead. "Human rules don't apply to pack."

His finger grazes my breast.

"Some of them do," I say. He makes me feel breathless and needy, and I'm not sure how I feel about that. He could be the king of orgasms, but he's also a wolf—and he's dominant. I don't need to borrow that kind of trouble—or fuck it.

"Why do you have kittens in your bathroom?" he asks, changing the subject on me. He rubs the top of Houdini's head again, and the shameless little creature stops hissing and starts purring.

"He likes you." Ignoring the way that finger of his isn't touching just the cat would be prudent.

"Magic fingers." I catch the quick flash of a smile out of the corner of my eye. "I know my way around—"

"*Don't* say it," I order, stepping away to set Houdini back down in the box. I don't need to hear Jace say the word *pussy*, because… yeah. He'll say it, and we'll both think about the available pussies in the room, and I don't need to imagine Jace thinking about my vagina. Houdini protests when I set him down, and I predict he'll make another break for it. I need to get out of this small space. Maybe with fifteen feet—or an entire state—between me and Jace, my libido will let my brain start thinking again.

"You didn't answer my question," he says, holding the bathroom door open for me. That means I'll have to walk down the hallway with him at my back—and I don't think the position is an accident. "You said you know all you need to know about me, so tell me what you know."

"You ride a bike. You belong to a motorcycle club. You're really good at hurting people, and right now you answer to the Jones Alpha, who also happens to be your brother."

I call the words over my shoulder. Funny how quietly he walks. I know he's behind me—the nerve endings in my body appear to be one big Jace radar—but I can't hear him move. I also can't decide whether his silence is unnerving or impressive.

I head for the kitchen. My stomach is hitting my backbone. I didn't make time for lunch, and unless my kitchen has miraculously sprouted groceries, I'm looking at kitten food or microwave pizza. Except when I step inside, I've grown a third option. A cardboard box filled with Chinese takeout cartons sits on my counter and I must have been really tired not to have smelled that—it smells heavenly. My stomach promptly growls in agreement. Real food. The kind that encompasses all four food groups and that doesn't require a microwave. Food is way better than sex.

"You brought food?"

"I'm gonna take care of you, sweetheart."

Well. Okay, then.

I don't want to fight with him, not when I could be eating and he's clearly made an effort (not that I know why—I'm a sure thing thanks to my dad), so I bite my tongue and get out plates. When we each have a full load, he tugs me back out into the living room and down onto the couch.

If it had been up to me, I'd have picked the table, but this is kind of nice. My couch isn't big, and Jace's thigh presses up against mine as we eat. He doesn't say much at first, so I concentrate on dinner.

When I'm so full I can't eat another bite, I set my plate on the coffee table and curl up. Jace also brought a bottle of wine and a six-pack of beer. Normally I don't drink (and okay, I prefer those frozen cocktail drinks that resemble milkshakes with alcohol), but I let him pour me a glass of red and then he brings the bottle with him. And since he makes me more than a little nervous, one glass leads to two. Or possibly three. I'm a lightweight, and now he knows it too. I also still don't know why he's come over, but I plan to find out.

"Did my dad send you?" Things feel more than a little awkward between us, what with my dad offering me like I'm some kind of commodity (which, in his mind, I am) and Jace seeming willing to take him up on the offer. I suspect the operative word is *seeming*, because Jace doesn't take orders, and I instinctively trust him. That trust part is probably stupid, but my wolf likes him. *She* doesn't think he's going to hurt us intentionally—and she doesn't want to hear all the ways he could accidentally hurt us.

Jace shakes his head. "Came over because I wanted to."

Oh. I finish my wine while I think that one over. I don't have any experience dating, thanks to my dad, but I'm pretty certain that wasn't what Jace meant. So I take a guess.

"Your day wasn't complete until you'd committed felony B&E?" Since I hadn't given him a key, there is only one way he could have gotten in.

He looks unrepentant. "Told you you needed new locks. Anyone could get in here. You got a weapon?"

Nope. My dad hadn't trusted me with one after what happened to Bolt. Not that I'd shot the wolf or anything—just not pulled him out of the bayou and away from the gators—but my dad knew something had happened. He just hadn't been able to prove it, and it had been more convenient for him to keep me around in one piece. Gave him an opportunity to play the mating game twice.

"I've got pepper spray," I volunteer, and he gives me a look. We both know pepper spray won't stop a werewolf. It's kind of like putting Tabasco on chicken—except I'm the meal in question.

"Can you shift?" He sets my wine glass on the table and pulls me into his side casually. I stiffen up as soon as I make full body contact with him. Food I can handle, but cuddling with Jace is too much. I still don't know what he wants, but it's undoubtedly more than I can afford to give him. Even if the scent and feel of him is nice…

"Relax," he grunts, like a one-word command is all it takes. Must be nice to be him—bigger, stronger, and in charge.

Since I'm clearly not going anywhere—and my wolf craves touch like most wolves—I let my head fall onto his chest. I can hear the steady beat of his heart beneath my cheek, and then his arm curls around me. With anyone else, I would feel trapped. Funny how Jace makes me feel safe instead. Safe—and special.

"I can shift," I murmur, mentally debating where to put my hands. I finally settle on tucking them beneath my cheek. "I just prefer to stay human."

If I had my way—which looks about as likely as snow in California in July—I'd never shift again.

"Big Red or one of the Breed teach you basic self-defense skills?"

I blame what comes out of my mouth next on the wine. "Fighting them makes it worse."

He must know what the *it* is because he curses. A really obscene, graphic curse. I've been forced to do that too, so I just wait for him to be finished.

"You should know how to defend yourself," he says when he runs out of curse words. "I'll teach you."

"You?"

"Me," he growls. "Someone's gotta do it."

"Do I need to defend myself from you?" The words kind of hang in the air between us, the subject we've both been dancing around. My dad wants the two of us to mate, and what my dad wants, he orders and gets. It's that simple. Self-defense lessons are a moot point.

"I don't want to hurt you," he snaps, but that isn't the question I asked.

"Then don't," I growl back. His fingers tighten in my hair.

"You realize what I could do to you?" His dark gaze bores into me. "We're alone, Keelie Sue, and I outweigh you. I could be on you in seconds. Nobody to hear, nobody to help—you want to let me do what I've been fantasizing about since the last time I got you on a bed alone?"

I should run for the door, even if it *is* my own damned door and he's the intruder. Instead, I open my mouth, and the question just kind of pops out. "What do you fantasize about?"

He looks me straight in the eye, and I fight the urge to drop my gaze. To admit he's the dominant one, and I'm the submissive.

"Fucking you. I'm gonna strip you, hold you down, and fill you up. Any way I can, I'm gonna get inside you. I'm gonna make you like it too, like it so much that you're begging for me."

Begging sure isn't on *my* fantasy bucket list. I've done enough of that to know it isn't sexy. "That sounds more like a plan than a fantasy."

The slow smile he gives me is part scary, part sexy as hell. It's the look of a predator spotting his prey. He has me, and we both know it. "Let's find out."

He moves, reaching for me, and he's right. I can't stop him. He takes me down to the floor, like the animal he claims to be, twisting so that he takes the brunt of the fall. For a long moment I stare down at him, then he rolls and pins me beneath him. My head whirls, both from the wine and my sudden change in positions.

"Gotcha," he whispers roughly, his fingers tangling in mine.

When did I start *liking* Jace Jones?

And where did this urge to lick him all over come from?

He rocks against me, pressing his dick into my front.

Okay. When he does things like that, my urge to lick makes perfect sense.

# JACE

I'm done with the games. I want to fuck her again, and she isn't saying no. Since we need to be clear on the *yes, do me again* portion of events, however, I lean down, forcing her to meet my gaze.

"If you want me to leave, tell me now."

Just in case she has any doubts about the next item on my date-night agenda, I slide my dick up her denim-covered pussy. She needs to lose the pants. Since she doesn't say anything, I figure I have the green light. It's okay with me if she's a little shy. Her experience with her daddy's wolves hasn't been good, and she's still learning she can trust me.

Letting go of her hands, I drop down her body. She has a gorgeous, compact body, all sweet curves. When I settle between her legs, she makes a little squawking noise as if I've surprised her. She'll just have to get used to me, and right now I really, really want a taste of her pussy. Just so I can see if she's even sweeter than I remember.

I pop the button on her jeans, and tug. "Off."

She blinks at me, the wine clearly still doing a number on her brain, but then she lifts her butt so I can pull her pants off and toss them away. Just to be certain, I inhale, but I don't smell fear. My girl smells aroused.

Her panties are cute, a little white lacy number with blue polka dots and a pink bow that are the perfect target for my tongue.

"I like these." I circle the bow with my finger.

She makes another noise and kind of tries to close her legs. Too bad for her I'm already between them. She doesn't stand a chance against two hundred pounds of wolf, as I tried to tell her before. Guess we'll play show-and-tell now.

Her fingers flutter here and there, like she's trying to decide if she wants to hide her goodies from me, or do something else. Since I'm up for making suggestions, I grab her hands and set them on my shoulders.

"Jace—"

"I'm listening." I am, too. If she has a list of all the places she wants me to kiss, or the dirty things she needs me to do to her? I'm her fucking wolf, that's for sure.

"We shouldn't—"

"You don't have to do anything. I'm gonna take care of everything." I mean it, too. While sinking my dick inside her tops my current wish list, I also intend to make this good for her. She's had a shit deal in life, and I absolutely want to kiss her better. The way I see it, all she has to do is enjoy. I'll do all the rest.

I'm practically a Boy Scout and she can pin the medal to my goddamned chest later. First, I have my mate to kiss.

I ease down a little further, grabbing one of her throw pillows and tucking it under her head. Probably should take this to the bedroom, but she hasn't invited me there yet, and I don't want to wait. Feels like I've been waiting about a century for this anyway.

"You're gorgeous," I tell her, although gorgeous is an understatement. Her panties frame the prettiest pussy I've ever seen, a sweet mound with hair the color of caramel. Thanks to the peek-a-boo lace stuff decorating the front of her panties, I have no doubts about that at all.

She wriggles, and that's my invitation right there. I press my mouth to the top of her mound, hooking my thumbs in the lacy straps over her hips, and she makes another one of those sounds I love so much.

"You're loud." I can't keep the satisfaction out of my voice, and a pretty pink flush spreads over her cheeks and down. Best. Fucking. Moment. Ever. Her white panties make me feel dirty as hell. I know I'm pushing her, taking her outside her comfort zone, because no matter what those other bastards did to her, they did it for themselves. They hadn't made sure she enjoyed it, and for that alone I'd have to fucking kill them.

Just not right now.

Two quick jerks, and the straps holding her panties together break. I tear her panties off because why the hell not? Cute as they are, I want what's underneath more. Her scent hits me, all arousal and sweet female, and it feels so fucking right my wolf wants to howl.

She babbles something that almost sounds like words, her nails digging into my shoulders hard. I really want to listen, but all I know are that the sounds coming out of her mouth aren't *no* or *stop* or even *you goddamned bastard*. So we're good.

I lick her. Do it nice and slow too, giving her a chance to get used to me because I'm such a gentleman. She's slick, all wet and juicy, and now I'm the one groaning. She's still blushing, although I don't know what she has to be embarrassed about. She's beautiful, and I sure don't mind knowing she wants me. I'll make this good for both of us.

I part her pussy with my fingers, holding her open for my mouth and exploring her with my fingertips. Trying to be gentle almost kills me, but she rewards me with a moan. A moan that gets louder when I drag my fingers up, the work-roughened skin pulling at her. She's sensitive as shit, and I love that.

Love a whole lot about her, if I'm honest.

I cover her with my mouth, claiming every inch of her that I can. I might not get in her head or her heart—and stupid bastard that I am, I kinda want to be there too—but I'll own her pussy. I eat her like a starving man, licking and tonguing.

She tastes so goddamned good. Not like I haven't

gone down on a female hundreds, fucking thousands, of times before, but Keelie Sue is different. Probably could have made a list that fills a book, but I'm too busy getting lost in those sweet little sighs that she makes. Then she gets a little lost herself, trying to grab my hair and drag me exactly where she needs me most.

Time for her reward. I rub her hard with my tongue, shoving into her body with my fingers. Give her three, and she takes me easily, her body melting around mine right before she clenches around me. Moaning and squirming, she comes on my tongue, and I love every fucking second of it. Might love her too, but I'm not going there, not right now. Not with my tongue deep in her pussy, and her knees tight around my head. I'll figure it out later.

She collapses back on the floor with a little mewl. I've turned my mate into a boneless heap, so I've finally done something right. A few seconds later and I know that this taste of her is all I'll get tonight. She lets out a little snore, half a bottle of wine and one hell of an orgasm catching up with her.

I probably should be pissed off because my dick is iron hard and it isn't getting any satisfaction tonight that doesn't come from my palm. Instead, I grin like an idiot and scoop her up off the floor. I'll tuck her into bed and then I'll stay for a few minutes. I can have that much, right? Time enough later to get going, get back on my bike, and start kicking pack ass. I stop to swipe her torn-up panties from the living room floor on my way to put her in bed because I deserve a souvenir.

I'm not going to lie. Best moment of my life. Ever.

6

KEELIE SUE

W HEN I WAKE UP the next morning, my head is fuzzy from too much wine and I'm alone. The headache is only proof that last night was a mistake. Dear God. Jace had gone down on me again, and I'd loved every wicked minute of his attention—right up until I'd fallen asleep on him. On the floor. Naked from the waist down, my memory supplies oh-so-helpfully, because the humiliation and embarrassment aren't complete until I remember *that* particular detail.

Shoot. Me.

I have a bad feeling I didn't drunk-walk my way to bed either. I'm completely naked underneath the sheets when I take inventory. I hadn't been *that* drunk, I remind myself. Just slightly incapacitated. So we had sort-of sex, I came, and then I passed out. I can probably make it up to Jace, if he's still talking to me.

My phone buzzes with an incoming text on the

nightstand, and when I automatically grab it, I discover Jace left me a bottle of water, two Advils, and a note. *I fed the pussies.*

Not touching that one.

The text on my phone doesn't improve my morning either. My dad has sent an address and a terse order to *Get your ass over there. Fang's got something for you.*

Great. I don't want to run around with any other wolves, and Fang tops my own personal no-fly list. The man is mean as hell, and he's ambitious. The combination doesn't bode well for what's left of my morning.

Sure enough, when I pull into the warehouse's parking lot, the GPS cheerfully announcing that I've reached my destination, Fang leers at me and swings off his bike.

"Got something for you, baby girl."

Oh joy. I roll down my window and look at him expectantly. Naturally he laughs and pats his thigh.

"I'm not gonna make it that easy. You come over here and ask me nicely for your present."

As opposed to staying in the car—with the engine running? I know which option I prefer. When I don't budge, Fang smiles. God, he's a toothy bastard. He also knows he has me, because whatever my father has sent, I need to collect it. Reluctantly I get out of the car and trudge over to him. When I try to stop a good two feet away, he reaches out and wraps his hand around my upper arm hard enough to bruise.

"You listen, and things don't have to be so hard." He gives my arm a little pinch, then lets go. I fight the urge to turn and run. My wolf wants to duck, tuck us low against the ground.

Fang reaches a hand under his shirt, and for a moment my breath catches. I can't do this again. When he pulls his hand out, he's holding a gun. I don't know my firearms, but this one is small, compact, and downright lethal-looking.

"For Saturday night," he tells me. "In case shit gets out of control. You know how to shoot?"

I swallow hard. "My dad okay this?"

Fang shakes his head. "Told him I had a present for you. Kind of like a courting gift. Shit's gonna get crazy on Saturday, and I can't stick by your side the whole time."

I have no idea when he got the idea that I'd welcome his company, but this is a side of Fang I've never seen before. I nod slowly, and take the gun from Fang. He won't let me leave without it, and besides… I can always shoot him with it. That idea appeals to me more than it should.

While I try to figure out what to do with the gun— my purse is on the front seat of my car and I absolutely am *not* shoving a loaded weapon down the back of my pants—Fang pats his arm. "You notice anything different, baby girl?"

In general, I try to avoid Fang and my father's wolves. No point in borrowing trouble. Still, I look instinctively, and that's when I realize that he's wearing a leather cut. A cut with the Breed's colors on it— my father must have patched him in. My day is now complete.

"Congratulations," I say. Pissing him off by not acknowledging his promotion would be stupid.

"Gonna throw down for you at the ball," he announces, his fingers tightening on my arm. "Make you my old lady and my mate."

Over my dead body.

He strokes my forearm, and my stomach lurches.

"Thanks for the gun," I say, wondering how fast I can get out of there—and if it's going to be fast enough. Fang makes me nervous.

"Boom." He laughs, throwing a leg over his bike. "We're gonna have fireworks on Saturday."

## JACE

Feels like I've spent a fucking eternity waiting for Saturday night. After I ate out Keelie Sue and put her to bed—which turned out to be a pretty awesome way to spend the night—Big Red kept me busy with club business. And when he wasn't trying to run my ass ragged, Cruz gave it a shot.

Two of the Breed wolves are in custody, and Cruz is understandably concerned about those brothers showing their true colors. It's not like we suddenly go furry at full moon, but being locked up doesn't sit well with a wolf, any more than being cut off from shifting does. Since neither of the two incarcerated Breed members are known for their ethics, I figure it's only a matter of time before they decide to shift anyhow.

So it's been a long, shit week when I pull up in front of Keelie Sue's place, the roar of the bike's pipes bouncing off the walls. A couple of the neighbors stick their heads out, get a good look at me, and then think better of whatever it is they were planning to say. Keelie Sue rents half of a ramshackle duplex. The outside hasn't been painted in longer than she's been alive, and the front porch sags to the right. But the morning glory and honeysuckle eating up the railings is real pretty, and the place smells like her.

I wait a minute and then, when she doesn't pop out, swing off the bike to go fetch her. There are plenty of things I don't know about her yet. Like if she's always on time, always late, or somewhere in between. After tonight we'll be mates, and then I'll have all the time in the world to learn things about her. I'm looking forward to it, truth be told. Almost more than I am to getting inside her sweet, tight hole.

Almost.

I'm no fucking saint.

When she opens the door and steps out, I about short-circuit. She wears those skinny jeans that look painted on, except the denim is soft, like maybe they're her favorites. I like the black halter top even better, especially as I'm pretty certain she's skipped a bra. She's put her hair up in a ponytail and a pair of long, sparkly earrings brush her bare shoulders. If we weren't expected, I'd scoop her up and carry her back inside. I didn't want to press my luck after she let me have a taste earlier in the week, but damn... she looks good. I should have brought flowers or something.

I mean, I've brought her a present, but I hadn't planned on whipping it out at her front door. I finger the teeny, black velvet box I'd shoved inside the front pocket of my jeans. Stupid to be sentimental, but I'm hoping our mating means more to her than pack politics, and so I've picked out a little something for her. I'm not sure if I should give it to her now, or wait until later when we're alone. Since I like the thought of her naked and wearing nothing but my ring, waiting it is.

"I guess you're ready to get going," she says, her purse bumping against her hip as she starts down the steps. I sniff, but can't quite figure out her scent. She smells anxious and more than a little nervous, and I have no idea how to fix that. Gotta give it a shot though.

"You ever drive a bike?" I pat the seat.

She gives me a look, but she comes over. "I know how to ride."

I've never let anyone else drive my bike. I don't give up control. Ever.

"We're gonna be late," I warn her. "So we should get going. If you wanna drive, you drive."

"And my driving would be a pity," she says dryly.

I don't want to force her into anything, but I'm not the worse deal out there. I'll take care of her, and I damned certain won't hurt her. She enjoys my kisses, and I have plenty more of those. I'm not sure what it would take to banish the hesitation from her eyes, but I want to be the man who does it. Keelie Sue is all kinds of special.

I back off so she can swing onto the bike, then as soon as she's seated, I get on behind her. The seat isn't really built for two, even if she's a tiny thing. As soon as I get back on, my legs hug her hips. This is good, because my legs protect hers from the pipes and any-thing the tires might kick up.

I hand her the helmet, and she twists back to look at me.

"You're really going to let me be in charge?"

Feels like she's asking a dozen other questions, but what am I supposed to say? "I'm all yours."

Three words, but I mean each one in every way pos-sible. I'm definitely hers tonight. Hell, I've been hers since I saw her, and I don't anticipate that changing.

Ever.

She nods and opens the bike up. A little tentative, but she knows what she's doing as she noses us out onto the street. I slide my hands around her waist and hang on. Right then, I'm happy to go wherever she wants.

KEELIE SUE

If we weren't headed to my dad's mating ball, the night would be perfect. The full moon lights up the road, and the bayou has never looked prettier. The

99

light spills across the dark surface in bright silver ribbons, the trees forming a lacy canopy overhead. I could drive all night.

Jace wraps his arms around me and holds on. His thumb rubs back and forth over my belly, his legs gripping mine as he leans into the dips and curves with me. His bike is a thing of beauty too, the machine eating up the miles with sleek power. I feel the vibrations through every inch of my body.

Just for fun, I let the throttle out, pushing the bike to see what she can do. There may be only one way to go, just one choice, but Jace lets me make it at my own speed. All too soon we reach the place where my dad has decided to stage his party. We're miles out of town and deep in the bayou where no one can hear or see what happens, no accidental witnesses to the Breed's debaucheries. By the time we pull up, the bonfire has reached impressive heights, and the wolves have already tapped the kegs.

I ease back on the throttle, killing the engine and coasting toward the line of bikes where two prospects stand guard and act as valet parkers. Jace is off the bike before I've come to a complete stop. Guess our ride is over. He certainly won't want the others making a big deal of the way he's arrived.

He takes my hand and leads me toward the bonfire. We're close to the flames, the heat pinking my face, before I see the other women. My dad wasn't kidding—he'd rounded up six women from somewhere. I don't know where he found the old metal cage he stuck them in, but it's hard to miss. Fear rolls off them in waves, almost drowned out by the lust and pheromones coming off my dad's wolves. The bastards eat up their captives' terror.

Those girls are supposed to be long gone. Jace promised to help. No. That wasn't it. Now that I think about it, he promised to do something—and that covers plenty of territory, and none of it is guaranteed to bust those girls free. Trusting him was probably a mistake.

I look at him.

He looks right back at me, and I fight the urge to drop my gaze. He might be dominant, but some things merit standing up for.

"You promised." The words fly out of my mouth, even louder than I intended, and heads swing our way. "You were going to take care of them. You said you kept your promises."

Promises made in bed don't count. I know that, and yet I trusted Jace. I'm so stupid.

Jace stalks toward me, his long legs eating up the clearing. I can't interpret his smile. "Working on it," he snarls, stopping in front of the fire. "In the meantime, why don't you come over here with me? We'll announce our happy mating news to the pack."

The smile he gives me is downright predatory, and then he pats his thigh like I'm some kind of dog. The man should sue whoever taught him his communication skills.

He sucks.

"Keelie Sue Berard," Jace says, and I just know the whole pack hears him. My world kind of stands still, waiting for the next words out of his mouth. It's stupid, because this isn't what I wanted, not really, but my body tenses in anticipation. "I claim you as my mate."

Behind him, my dad mimes cocking a gun with his thumb and forefinger. He looks pleased, but he should because the bastard is getting the son-in-law he picked out for himself. Jace holds out his hand, waiting for me to place mine in his.

Do it.

Don't do it.

My dad growls when I hesitate, his gaze skewing toward the group of frightened human women. I wanted to set them free, but I counted on Jace to do it.

101

He failed, but maybe a diversion will work almost as well. Refuse Jace, cause a commotion, and maybe the girls can make a run for it. And maybe nuclear weapons or an entire SEAL team will rain down from the sky. They are every bit as on their own as I am. Jace is just like my dad. He isn't a white knight riding to the pack's rescue—or mine.

I shoot him a tight smile, and his eyes narrow. Yeah. That's romance right there. *Not.* I have Fang's present, however, so maybe there *is* something I can do. I swallow, staring at Jace. Willing him to step up, to do something.

He frowns instead. "Everything okay?"

"Not yet," I tell him and reach for the gun.

## JACE

Keelie Sue opens that ridiculous little orange purse slung over her shoulder. The thing is more fringe than bag. I don't know what women carry around with them. Don't really want to know, truth be told. But if I was forced to guess, I'd bet the contents were probably the same as the stuff I carried around. Except maybe for a lipstick or two. I don't do that shit.

Turns out I'm right. I carry a gun—and so does Keelie Sue.

Of course I don't point mine at her, and that's a big fucking difference.

"Sorry, but I'm off the market," she says to me, stepping closer to the caged women. "You and my dad can console each other."

She sounds like she means it too, which makes

even less sense. She's never said that she doesn't want our mating, and then she asked me to fix the problem of the human females. I agreed. I've already arranged with Eli to spring them, and one of our other brothers has moored a boat by the water's edge. We'll open the cage, lead the girls to the boat, and then they'll be free and clear. When the fuck did Keelie Sue decide to stop trusting me?

Unlike her old man, I've been nothing but nice to her. I've had more than one opportunity to hurt her, and I've chosen to be *nice*. My mistake. And if I have all these unfamiliar, warmer emotions for her? Yeah. I've got the memo on that too. Apparently, I can keep my *feelings* to myself. Along with my dick, my hands, and my heart.

"Sorry's not going to cut it, sweetheart." I take a step toward her, running options in my head. She's just disrespected me in front of the entire pack, and that's going to require some serious damage control.

Fuck.

Honestly, I have no idea what kind of relationship we have, but I know one thing. That relationship had just gone south. Not that I need her to bring me roses, but bullets are hard to misinterpret. She threatened to hurt me when she should have had my back. So I'll kill the bastard who put her in this position, rescue her damsels in distress, and then she and I will have ourselves a talk. Keelie Sue has a lesson to learn tonight, and I'm just the wolf to teach her.

"Listen to your mate, girl," Big Red growls behind her. He's a shitty Alpha. He should call me out in a fight, go head to head with me to settle the animosity brewing between us, but he isn't that kind of guy. He fights dirty, and he uses others to get what he wants. He tried to bribe me with Keelie Sue, and I let him.

*Sorry*, Keelie Sue mouths again, and I kinda am too.

The only part of tonight that's gonna go as planned

for her is the part where she gets fucked.

I shift. She reaches for the latch on the cage, the muzzle of the gun panning the assembled wolves. No fucking clue what she thinks she's doing or who she intends to threaten, but if I'm gonna be Alpha, that means I have wolves to protect—and that includes Keelie Sue. I go for Big Red.

Bastard either isn't expecting it, or he's been too into watching the sideshow he engineered. I crash into him hard, pinning him to the ground. I sink my wolf's teeth into his throat and tear. Stretching out the kill appeals—his job was to protect Keelie Sue and instead he repeatedly put her in danger—but she's already flung open the latch on the cage and scrambled away from the ring of wolves closing in to watch our fight. She'll be deep in the bayou in minutes, and it's dark. She's alone, and all kinds of bad shit can happen to her out there.

So I make it quick. I tear into Big Red's throat like he's the steak and I'm the carnivore. The bayou's sandy banks soak up his blood, hungry for more, and I feed it Big Red. I fasten my jaws on his throat, crushing whatever I haven't ripped to fucking shreds. Big Red groans and almost manages the shift, fur running over his body as he reaches deep for whatever he has left. Isn't happening. My wolf and I hold him down in the dirt and bite deeper.

## KEELIE SUE

I've rejected Jace's mate claim.

My stomach heaves and twists, trying to turn itself

inside out. I don't have to look behind me to know that Jace will be on me before I can blink. I've disrespected him and he wants pack leadership—he can't leave my challenge unanswered.

I run, but something pulls my feet to a stop, something chains me to the spot and makes me look. Like Lot's stupid, regretful, can't-leave-it-alone wife, I pause and take in the fight.

The wolves roar and howl, but no one stops me. They're too busy watching Jace kill our Alpha and step into his place. He has the pack—now all he needs is me, and not because I'm his golden ticket to running the pack anymore. He's top dog now—or will be in minutes—and he doesn't need me. I'm going to be the moral of the what-happens-to-wolves-who-piss-on-their-opponents story.

I'll pay a high price for my shot at freedom. I know that. Jace won't show me any mercy. It won't matter that he's had his mouth between my legs, or that he's touched me with surprising gentleness. I rejected his claim and I sort of pulled a gun on him. Frankly, I don't know why I'm not dead now, but I'll take the chance and run.

An old wolf told me once that the first werewolf packs ranged over medieval Europe, treating the continent like their own personal playground. Eventually some of the wolves crossed the ocean, tired of the brutality of that life and looking for a new start. I can't begin to imagine what their former lives must have been like, because these guys definitely put the *brute* in brutal.

Jace is sending a message of his own right now and there's absolutely nothing civilized about it. Two hundred pounds of wolf pin my dad to the ground. Whatever Big Red's plans were, he underestimated Jace, because Big Red doesn't even get the chance to shift. Snarls fill the air, blood splattering on the floor as the wolf tears Big Red's throat wide open. I've seen TV shows, and I've witnessed violence plenty of times more personal and close up. But in all of those assaults, the weapons were usually less personal—guns, chains, nunchakus, and a truly creative variety of improvised homemade explosives. Fists were sometimes used in the commission of a crime, and gouging, hitting, and mixed martial arts were all possibilities, but those moves had nothing on the scene unfolding in front of me.

I'm not a veterinarian or a surgeon, but it seems clear who's winning—and who's losing. Jace is about to kill my dad.

The faces of the men ringing the combatants tells a different story. They're fighters and perfectly okay with the battle playing out in front of them. Their world. Their rules. My dad tried to get that through my head, and I know Jace agrees with him on this one point. Looking at the shifters filling the clearing, I also know my decision to break free from the pack is the right one. These hard men are sun-bronzed bayou bad boys on the outside, pretty to look at in the way the lethal predators at the zoo are. All that man-killing grace prowling around, looking back at you through the glass, makes you glad for the moats, bars, and inches of plexiglas between you and them. Without out those safety precautions, you're prey and the only thing to do is run.

Since the first step is always the hardest, or so the cliché goes, I settle for ducking along the edge of the bayou. Twenty yards to the trees. Forty or fifty steps more, and then I'll be on my way to freedom.

"*Chere*, you don' listen too well." There's no mistaking the rough amusement in Eli Jones's voice—or the stop sign that is his large, muscled body. Forward momentum sends me slamming into him, my brain yammering its *cease and desist* order too late to my feet. His hands steady me even as he yanks me up against his body.

"Sue me," I mutter. I know better than to argue—hello, wasted breath—when Eli places a hand on my head and shoves me to the ground. I guess the move counts as protective and I should be appreciative, but now I have an almost pornographic close up of his blue jeans and steel-toed boots. He's a good-looking man, but the wolf I'm interested in is his brother, Jace.

Who is undoubtedly coming after me to teach me a lesson.

"I'm out of here," I explain just in case he's mistaken my departure for something else.

"I don' think so." He pins me in place, the move casual-like despite the lack of give in his arm. "You stay here until I can take you home. First I've got to lead those girls down to the boat."

"What?" A beer bottle shatters on the ground nearby, showering me with sticky splinters of glass and drenching me in the unpleasant aroma of stale beer.

"Jace asked me to get those girls out of here. Said you wanted them safe, and he did too." Eli stares down at me, obviously aware that there's no good reason for me to be lurking on the edges of a werewolf challenge when I've just rejected one of the main players. He clearly believes my loyalties are a big-ass question mark.

He's not wrong.

Jace had really intended to do something for the girls? I look backward. Across the clearing, both combatants are now naked, bloody, *human*. They've shifted back from wolf form. Jace's cold, hard gaze meets mine as he snaps my dad's neck in a casual show of domination. Power radiates off him—and he's pissed. Holy gods, but he's mad. It shouldn't also be sexy as hell, but apparently I have a thing for bad boys and my new mate is the best of the worst. He gets my panties wet and my body going whenever I'm around him, and he knows it.

"Trust is a good thing," Eli drawls, following my gaze. "You might want to work on it."

I'm not going to get the chance.

Jace drops my dad's body. Somebody tosses him a pair of jeans and he pulls them on, watching me the whole time. He doesn't try to pretend to be anyone or anything other than what he is: our new Alpha with the body of the dead Alpha at his feet and surrounded by his pack wolves. I love that strength, but after tonight he'll be as done with me as he is with the dead wolf on the ground.

"Jace is gonna paddle your butt. Stay put." Eli doesn't stick around for my answer. A roar goes up from the center of the clearing as the wolves surge toward Jace. Slapping a hand on the bike, Eli vaults lightly over the seat and closes in on the cage. The Jones brothers don't back down from a fight and tonight is no exception. He fights hard and he fights mean, laying into any wolves standing between him and the women remaining in the cage. Guess they've found their hero after all, which leaves me with only one smart thing to do…

*Run.*

7

JACE

KEELIE SUE PUSHES THROUGH the crowd of wolves witnessing my challenge, making for the bayou. I know Eli is keeping an eye on her, which is the only thing keeping me fucking sane at the moment. She looks like crap, her eyes big and wide as she registers the shit storm she's kicked off. I've just taken out her dad in a challenge, and that makes me the Breed's new Alpha.

*Her* Alpha.

Eli starts hauling women out of the cage Keelie Sue unlocked. He'll make sure they get somewhere safe too. Won't stop them from running their mouths about what happened here or what they've seen—Big Red's wolves haven't been shy about changing since they saw the girls as fresh meat—but I'll deal with that later.

I have bigger problems. Cruz appears seemingly

out of nowhere and blocks my path. Guess Eli enlisted him as werewolf-bride rescue back up.

"You need to get the hell out of here," I snap. "My pack, my business."

Cruz curses, taking in for the first time the dead body I've left behind me. I tore Big Red's throat out, and that kind of kill is messy. I have blood on my hands, my chest, my legs.

"Big Red's dead. The pack's mine." Too late for regrets.

"Which is a good thing, truth be told," Cruz says. "Big Red was a crazy bastard, and he needed to be stopped. You can let Keelie Sue go with the rest of the girls."

"I'm going after my mate," I say pointedly. "I'm gonna teach her a lesson."

"You don't wan' to hurt her." Cruz lays a hand on my arm and I shake it off.

"Hurting her is never part of the equation."

Cruz slams his own hand against the palm of a nearby tree. "Some advice? Take five and wash the blood off. You killed her old man, and you don' want to rub her face in it."

"Fuck you," I say easily, the words belying the urgency tearing through me. He isn't my Alpha anymore—I'm his fucking equal in the pack hierarchy, and every inch of me, man and wolf, screams that I should chase down my errant mate and teach her exactly who is the boss.

Fucking sucks that Cruz has a point about the blood.

I shift back into my wolf and head toward the bayou, his laughter ringing in my ears.

## KEELIE SUE

One minute I'm alone, reaching for the boat and calculating the odds that I might actually make it out of the bayou. Hope isn't a strategy, I remind myself—but a boat is. The next minute a freight train of pissed off, aggressive werewolf slams into me.

So much for hope. The world tilts as the air vacates my lungs and I head for the ground. Jace shifts back to human as he takes me down, pinning my arms to my side, one leg thrown over mine. This time he doesn't try to take the hit for me. I land hard, my purse flying away as my back drives into the ground, my head bouncing off something that feels like a rock. Or a root. Don't know, doesn't matter.

If Jace wants tears or begging, he's out of luck, because all I can do right now is fight to breathe and not black out. It's over and I've lost. I did what I could to break free of the pack, and it still isn't enough. *Game over.*

I let my head fall back onto the ground. The stars swirl overhead like I'm riding a tilt-a-whirl. Jace has all the advantage now, and I have nothing.

"Why do you want to run from me?" He rolls, coming up on top and straddling me as he asks his question. His legs press against my hips hard, holding me in place. Not like I have anywhere to go now. With Big Red dead, I'm orphaned and unemployed in one stroke. And Jace wants to talk about our *mating*?

I concentrate on not puking, willing the world to stop swinging around me. Somehow my reasons for rejecting Jace don't seem so convincing anymore.

"You better talk to me," he growls, when the silence stretches on. Around us, the bayou gets back to business, and the cicadas resume their nighttime rhythm to the counterpart of the bullfrogs' bass.

I scan his face not sure what I hope to read there. Not sure why the menace written there kind of turns me on either, but he's strong, and I'm wolf at heart. His strength calls to me.

He doesn't want to hear that I maybe still find him attractive—or that I'm more than a little turned on by his chasing and catching me. "What can I say?"

"Start with the truth," he orders. "Why not take me as your mate?"

The world tilts again, so I close my eyes. It's easier that way, not having to look at Jace's face. I betrayed him. He thought *mate* when I thought *run away*, and if I still don't want to be any wolf's mate, well, Jace at least hasn't waved a gun in my face.

"I never wanted to kill you," I admit.

He doesn't so much as flinch. "All evidence to the contrary."

This is the wolf, the predator, the hunter. He isn't the man who held me and kissed me, who let my kittens scrabble up his leg and who teased me. That man is gone, and I've effectively killed *him* even if I haven't plugged the wolf with my bullet.

"I'd have given you everything," he tells me, and I have no idea what he means. Guess it doesn't matter, because he draws my hands up over my head, pinning them there with one hand. "You really think he'd have let his own daughter walk away from the pack?"

Maybe. Okay. Probably not. But I took the chance. Now I'm out of chances and done running. What happens next is up to Jace, and it actually feels good to cede control to him.

He lowers himself onto me, his hands still tangled with mine, stretching me out like some kind of virgin sacrifice to the gods. Except I'm no virgin—and there's nothing godlike about Jace. He's all devil.

He bites my lower lip, recalling me to the present. "You want to make me happy, sweetheart."

"Or?" I guess I'm finally done rolling over. My wolf whimpers, but she knows it too. We let Big Red take control, and it didn't work out. Jace probably won't be any better. He presses down harder and the move grinds his penis into me, the discomfort followed by an unexpected burst of pleasure. Something is definitely broken in my head if I'm thinking about sex now.

"Or things get ugly," he growls, but I don't mind the way his tongue laves the place where he bit me, easing the small sting. Pain. *Pleasure.* "Tell me where you got the gun from."

"Fang," I admit, and for a moment, it gets kind of hard to breathe. Jace's free hand, the one not pinning mine over my head, circles my throat, his thumb pressing against the pulse beating hard at the base of my throat. He scares me—and he turns me on. I don't know what to do with those feelings anymore so I keep right on talking.

"I met Fang and he gave me a gun," I continue. "He said it was a present, to keep me safe at the mating ball."

"You let him touch you?" Above me, Jace goes cold, menace radiating off his body. Guess he doesn't like Fang any more than I do. His hand on my throat tightens.

"No." I try to shake my head, but he holds me too tightly for that. "Fang's kind of a sick bastard. His girlfriends don't last long."

"Neither did your first mate." Jace's hand eases up, and I suck in a gulp of air. "I want to know if you fucked him."

"They had stuff in common," I admit. "But I'm not interested in Fang. He's no Mr. Wonderful."

"Good thing." Jace's eyes meet mine, full of hot possession. "I don't share my toys, sweetheart. You ask my brothers and they'll tell you. What's mine stays mine."

"You can't own a person," I feel compelled to point that out, although in all fairness, my dad owned the hell out of me. I just hadn't *liked* it.

"I own you," he says implacably. "Finish your story."

"I came out here tonight. I was supposed to accept your mating claim, but I didn't."

He makes a rough noise. "You couldn't reject me without witnesses?"

Have I done more than hurt his standing in the pack? I didn't think he really had any kind of feelings for me—other than the lustful kind—but he makes another rough sound, his thumb stroking over my pulse. I'm not sure if he wants to touch me—or hurt me. My body is getting all kinds of funny, mixed-up signals from my wolf. Then he lowers his mouth over mine. I'm not sure you could call it a kiss.

His mouth devours mine—the hot, hard contact my only anchor to reality. Spots swim in front of my eyes. It's easier to close my eyes and shut out everything but the rough press of his mouth as he thrusts his tongue against mine. He's savage in his kiss, his hand fisting my ponytail and yanking my head back so he can kiss me even deeper. Harder. And I love it. Sick and twisted as it is, he sets me on fire and makes me feel. The pleasure gets all mixed up with my body's panic at the lack of air, and I feel myself easing beneath him as the need to escape, to run, melts away and a sweet lassitude sets in.

A voice floats out of the darkness from somewhere behind Jace, and the hand on my throat falls away.

"You probably shouldn't kill her," Eli drawls.

"Probably not." Jace doesn't sound convinced though, and terror shoots through me again.

"Could stand up and let her go," Eli suggests. I hadn't realized he liked me—or maybe he just doesn't want to welcome me to the family. Maybe he realizes that letting me run would be the best thing for everyone. I'd be out of their lives, and Jace could get on with running the pack and finding himself a real mate.

Jace shoves to his feet. Sick as it is, I kind of miss the feel of his body on mine. I'm cold and tired. Getting up seems harder than scaling Everest, but the distant part of my head, the part that hasn't been chased, threatened, and half-kissed, half killed reminds me that I still need to put some distance between me and my wolf. I try too. I roll onto my side, hugging my knees to my chest, and I try. Guess I'm all out of tries, though, because I only manage to half get to my feet.

"She's mine," Jace says to Eli, and that's that.

Heat tears through me as he scoops me up from the ground. Would be nice if he consulted me about our plans, but I have to admit that I've pushed him too far. Nice Jace is gone, and instead I get the wolf. I let my head fall against his chest as he carries me to a boat. Eli must have brought it, because it isn't the pirogue I tried to use earlier. He sets me down on a seat.

"Stay there," he growls, tossing my purse onto the bench next to me. I'm kind of glad to see it, although worrying about my Visa card and my driver's license probably shouldn't even cross my mind. I have bigger problems.

I rest my head on the railing and stare out into the dark. The surface of the water breaks into a V-shaped ripple. Probably a gator there, and that brings back more memories. I guess I could handle being Jace's. It's certainly preferable to being dead. Or gator bait.

## JACE

I was nice. I tried dating. I fed her fucking kittens, and I listened while she talked. Keelie Sue needs to get a few things straight, and I'm just the wolf to teach her.

She doesn't challenge me in front of our pack. If she has a problem with me, she takes it to me. We'll work it out. Fuck, we can fight all day and all night too, if that's what she needs, but she doesn't challenge me, threaten me, or undermine my ass. That shows some serious lack of respect. And if one of my brothers had been close by when she whipped out that little handgun, she'd be dead. They have my back, and if she even appears to be gunning for me, she's a threat and they'll take her down.

Funny how I still hate the idea of her getting hurt.

Shit, I even stopped to pick up her purse because she'd probably want the bag or its contents. As I steer the boat out into the bayou, I can't stop watching or worrying about her either. Not sure when or how it happened, but at some point between Big Red offering her up to me like steak on a stick and her whipping a gun out and waving it around the mating ball, I've fallen for her.

Last thing I need are fucking *emotions*.

"Not too late to turn around," Eli mutters beside me. He's insisted on coming along, probably because he thinks I might kill Keelie Sue and later regret it. Or maybe he's afraid I *won't*. That's kind of a possibility too. As Baton Rouge's newest pack Alpha, I should be back at the mating ball cleaning house. At the very least, I should make a public example out of Keelie Sue.

If I could, I'd kill Big Red all over again. Keelie Sue should have come to me and let me take care of her dad. She should have trusted me to spring those girls.

I glare at the water rippling away from the boat. On a scale of zero to ten, her trust level is an insultingly negative number.

"I told her I'd take care of things," I grunt, steering the boat out into open water. The current runs deeper, faster here, and we pick up speed. Eli leans against the railing beside me, not taking his eyes off my mate. Guess he really doesn't trust her now, and I can't blame him.

"She coulda said no before tonight," he points out. "Could have asked for help. Could have *not* pulled her piece and threatened your wolves. She didn't do any of those things."

Fuck, but Eli is as blunt as a bullet himself. Good to know what he thinks and where he stands—he'll never bullshit me—but I don't like the truth. No big deal. I'll get used to it, right? Whatever feelings I have, Keelie Sue doesn't have the matching set. I might be thinking *like* and *lust*—because not even in my head am I touching the third L word, *love*—but she stinks of fear. Kinda don't like that either.

"Keelie Sue's got a lesson to learn," I agree, knowing she can hear me. She flinches, her fingers tightening on the edge of the boat. I keep an eye on her in case she decides to do something really stupid, like try to swim for shore, but she doesn't budge from where I set her.

"You don't have to be the one to teach it to her," Eli points out. I'm not sure what he's suggesting, but I won't tolerate anyone else touching Keelie Sue. "Maybe you should cut her loose, kinda like those girls in the cage."

"I'm keeping her." Kinda like hearing those words. Would be even better if she said the same about me, but I'll work on that. I read a bumper sticker once about today being the first day of the rest of my life. The way I see it, tonight is the first night in the rest of *our* lives. Keelie Sue isn't getting rid of me. I don't know what our time together meant to her—maybe it was just sex or a family obligation—but I'll make every second count from now on.

# KEELIE SUE

Jace didn't mess around. He pulls the boat into a private dock, barks a few words at Eli (who takes the wheel), and then he comes for me. Not like he has far to go— I'm still right where he put me, four feet away on the bench—but it's hard to look away. He's a big, rough outline storming toward me, and then his hands bite into my waist and I fly off the bench and over his shoulder. Guess the romance part of our relationship is definitely over.

His shoulder presses into my stomach, and I focus on not puking down his back. He swings us up onto the dock, then strides down it. Since he's providing the transportation and I'm too tired to do any more worrying tonight, I count planks. He needs to get a handyman out here or pick up a hammer because his dock is missing approximately every sixth board. I can see the dark bayou water through the gaps.

His heart pounds, the beat vibrating through his back, and his musky, feral scent surrounds me. He's pissed as hell, but he's also still Jace. And yeah, I want him. Maybe if we have sex things will straighten out somewhat with him. At the very least, it would give him an outlet for some of the frustration and anger surging through him.

He takes a set of porch steps two at a time and kicks open a door. Without turning on any lights, he strides down a hallway and then carries me upstairs, his booted feet eating up the stairs two at a time. When he reaches the landing, I try to shove up, but he slaps my butt. The contact has my blood humming and heat rising, because the attraction between us is crazy good. Emphasis on *crazy* at the moment.

"Don't," he growls. That one word covers a whole lot of territory.

We're in a bedroom, at least that's my conclusion from the big-ass four-poster bed. Looks kind of like the last bed he tied me to, but I don't recognize the room. A second later, I'm on my back on the bed, and he comes down over me.

"I bought furniture for you," he growls. Why he wants to talk about his furniture right now confuses me. After the stunt I pulled tonight, I'd think my opinions on his interior decorating are completely irrelevant. His face is scary as hell. Fierce. Focused on me. I've spent a lifetime hiding in plain sight of the pack, but when Jace looks at me, he *sees* me.

While I stare, he pulls his belt free of his jeans and lashes my hands to one of the posts. I buck instinctively. He wants to make me vulnerable when I need to be strong? Well, fuck him. The words sound so good in my head that I repeat them out loud.

"Fuck you."

"Working on it," he grunts, then pulls out a knife and slices my halter top off. Holy. Hell. The slick glide of the metal over my heat-flushed skin is... arousing. Apparently I'm all screwed up in my head because, yeah, I like it. I also still like him, which is a problem. Tossing the blade aside, he yanks my jeans down.

"You want to have sex now?" I can feel the hysterical laughter bubbling up inside me. It's so not a good time to have a fit of the giggles, but it's been one hell of a night, and I'll never, ever figure this wolf out.

His hands grab my ankles when I kick. "If you were trying to kill me, your aim sucks."

His doesn't. He shoves between my thighs, his hands going to the buttons on the front of his jeans. God. He still has his boots on. Funny how fear and lust can get so mixed up. My feelings for Jace bounce

119

around inside my head and my heart, all confused and stuck together. I rejected his mate claim, I tried to run from him—and I've never been so glad to fail in my life.

"Don't ever run from me again," he snarls.

"Don't push me." God help me, but I don't know where the words come from. Just that I'm tired of being told what to do, and how and when to do it. I might be wolf and pack, but I'm also human and I have *rights*. He can take his attitude and his orders and shove them both where the sun doesn't shine. Even if I don't want to kill him. "Get off."

I buck up again and he grins. A mean, pissed-off grimace. "Make me," he says.

He notches himself at my entrance, and frowns. He licks his fingers, getting them wet, and then coats me. His touch should be disgusting, a violation, but instead it feels primitive. Like a mark of his possession, and I don't care. I *want* this. Jace isn't nice, and this won't be sweet, slow Hallmark sex. It's going to hurt. I'll burn, my body stretching to accommodate his because he's bigger and stronger, but I'm going to make this all about me. *I'm* going to take *him*.

Step one? Make my intentions clear. "Do it," I demand.

He freezes, then growls. His dick pushes against my entrance, reminding me just how big he is. *Everywhere*. He slams into me, pushing deep inside my body. There's no keeping him out, and I don't want to. I shriek as he pounds into me, marking me from the inside out. I brace my legs on the mattress, canting my hips up to take him deeper. He tears inside me, and it feels so good I see stars. No. Not stars. I see *Jace*.

He rides me hard, and it's perfect. His big hands fist my hair, the rough tug echoing the harder, brighter pulse of pleasure in my pussy. He fills me up and takes me—and offers me something in exchange. Himself. I hate him. I… *love* him. He thrusts into me over and over, driving us both toward the edge. And when my orgasm explodes through me, I wrap my legs around his hips and seal him to me as my brain shuts down. All I can do is feel.

Jace over me. In me. Surrounding me with his big body, his power and heat. He comes with a rough groan, spilling himself deep inside me. We haven't used a condom I realize through the exhaustion creeping over my sated body. Guess it doesn't matter—it's not as if I have to worry about the future right now. For a long moment, he lies against me, and I run my foot up and down his leg.

When his breathing evens out, I hear the wet, intimate sounds of him pulling out of my body. He zips up and hesitates. For a moment, I'm not sure what's coming next, but then his big hands reach up and untie me, sliding his belt free and dropping the leather onto the floor beside the bed.

8

JACE

TWO DAYS LATER I walk into the clubhouse, and a couple of facts hit me right off. First, Keelie Sue isn't there. She's made her dislike of the pack clear, but apparently I'm stupid and harbored hopes. I wanted to see her come and stand with me, and now that obviously isn't happening. So, okay. I'll deal with her absence next. Second fact of the day that hits me? This place is mine now. I challenged the Alpha, and I won. His pack is mine, and they follow my orders.

Holy. Fuck.

I hadn't thought that one through. Okay, so I was pumped full of adrenaline, and Big Red hadn't endeared himself to me. Maybe I'd lost myself a little in my undercover role too. I'd come here and played the big bad wolf, but thing is—it isn't a role most of the time. I'm a mean bastard, and I'm good at hurting things. At hurting people. And while I might be able to fight worth a damn and I understand loyalty, I'm not so good at loving. I'm not expecting to look at the crowd of assembled wolves and feel anything other than possessive.

They're mine now.

If they get out of line, I'm responsible for kicking their asses.

The problem is that I'm also on the hook for keeping them safe and maintaining their all-round happiness. Fuck. I have no idea why I thought I could be an Alpha, but being anything but a *good* one stings. Somehow I'll have to figure it out. When I take another good look around the room, several of the older wolves stare back, assessing me. They don't step forward to challenge however. Guess they're okay with the change in leadership. I count, and come up with thirty wolves. We're missing five males.

Ware steps forward, tilting his dark head so I can see his throat. Black ink covers most of the skin there in harsh lines. Nothing soft about this wolf. "Alpha."

Funny how one word changes things so much. Ware isn't some cocksucker looking to shake things up. He's run with the Breed for a long time, and he's more than a pair of broad shoulders or a scarred face. He fought with Big Red, and I've gotten the distinct impression he disagreed with the dead Alpha on more than one occasion—and now he's transferred all that loyalty to me.

"We're gonna clean house," I announce, sweeping the assembled males with my gaze. "No more of this terrorizing the locals crap. The arms dealing is done, as are the drugs."

"You want us to go legal?" Ware straightens up, but he doesn't step back and he's setting the pattern for our relationship right there. Fine by me. I take a step forward, my shoulder slamming into his and forcing him to move. He grins, flashing his canines at me, but then moves back. The man is solid, and I appreciate that.

"Mostly." I glance over my wolves. I definitely have asses to kick there. "We're keeping our territory, and we're gonna run it, but some stuff's off the table."

I try to imagine what Cruz would say and come up blank. My big brother is the local sheriff—he'd shut down the Breed entirely. I'm not planning on running arms or drugs, and the reign of terror is definitely over, but there's still plenty about the MC that I love. Good stuff that I don't plan on losing.

"We're about riding and running," I say slowly, thinking it through. A few heads nod, so I kept talking. "We're about staying free. If no one gets up in our faces, we don't get in theirs."

"And if someone gives us trouble?" The question comes from a lanky, muscled wolf lounging in the corner, arms crossed over his chest. Blade earned his name because of his scary talent with knives and I have to wonder if he's planning a little backstabbing or throat-cutting from his corner.

"We kick his ass," I growl. "We're wolves, not kitty cats. You're gonna fill me in on all the details, and then I'm gonna decide which businesses we're keeping."

To my surprise, Ware nods slowly. "Losing the arms and the drugs will get law enforcement off our backs, and that's not a bad thing."

Guess I know where I'll be finding a second lieutenant. I make a mental note to tell the wolf he just scored himself a job interview and then get back to the business at hand.

"No more girls, either," I tell them, giving them another hard look. "You want pussy, you pay for it, you ask for it, or you work for it. No more kidnapping girls, and no more putting your dick where it's not wanted."

There's some grumbling at that, and I pay attention

to the wolves doing the complaining. They're my potential problem children right there. Neither Ware nor Blade bitch about the moratorium, although Blade shoots me a wicked grin.

"You calling time out on the pass-arounds too?" he asks.

Fucker is testing me. "If they're happy with the deal, not my place to complain, but we don't cage 'em up and they've got the right to walk away. Those are my rules. Anyone doesn't want to follow them, he's welcome to leave right now. You got a mate, you better make damned sure she's on board with staying with you. Big Red's dating service is closed."

The bastard has plenty to answer for, and I hope he rots in hell. On the edge of the group, Fang kind of stiffens up, but he keeps his mouth closed. Guess his ambition to earn a place for himself in the pack trumps his interest in my Keelie Sue. Good thing, too, or I'd kill him. Would kinda still like to, as a matter of fact.

"There going to be fallout from the mating ball?" Ware asks the question, but fuck if I know. Would help if I'd spoken with Cruz, but I'd been too busy chasing after Keelie Sue.

"We'll deal with it if and when it happens," I decide, "but right now we're clear. Eli here got the ladies out of the cage before the boys in blue spotted them, so that's one bullet dodged."

Ware nods. "They won't talk?"

"Up to them, but who's gonna believe them? There's no trail leading to us, and *werewolves kidnapped me* sounds pretty fucking far-fetched. As long as they keep their mouths shut, we leave them alone."

"And if they talk?"

"You bring it to me." Not that I have any idea what I'll do. Killing an innocent woman whose only real crime is being pretty and crossing paths with Big Red?

Yeah. That doesn't sit well. I'll have to figure something out when and if it happens.

We run through some more club business, and I lay out how it's gonna go. It'll take time to undo the mess Big Red made of the pack, but I have to figure it out. I'm not comfortable knowing that the other wolves are depending on me, but I've done the challenging and the killing too, so I'll have to figure out this next part as well. And I have to figure shit out with Keelie Sue.

Ware falls in with me when I leave the clubhouse. "Some of the wolves have mates," he observes. "Hasn't been my business what they do in their off-hours, but sounds like you're making it yours."

"Anyone wants to walk, she walks."

"Uh-huh." Ware pauses by a big black Harley. The brother's bike is as beat up as the wolf himself. Nothing pretty about the paint job or the scratched-up chrome, but it's built for speed. He'll eat up the road and then some. "You took Big Red's daughter."

The words hang in the air between us.

"She walks if she wants," I tell him, because it has to be said. I can't give my wolves one set of rules and then choose a different set for myself. Plus, it's the right thing to do. I'm not going to be another Big Red, even if just the thought of parting with Keelie Sue makes my wolf howl.

Ware swings a big leg over the bike. "You wanna ride?"

I do. I want to grab my bike, point it to the open road, and get the fuck out of here. I can feel responsibilities closing in on me, and even though I've chosen them for myself, it's kinda like getting hit with a shit tsunami. And truth is? I only have one place to be now, and that's on the road to Keelie Sue's. She didn't come and I have a few miles to accept that. I called the pack together, and she chose to be somewhere else.

When I took her as my mate, I overlooked something essential. What I got was her body, and sweet as that is, that's only a part of who Keelie Sue is. I didn't win her head—or her heart. She's mine—and yet not mine.

What. The. Fuck.

With a nod to Ware, I straddle my bike and let the engine rip, then ride out onto the street to open her up. The black ribbon of asphalt slips away beneath my boots, the wind stinging my face. Riding is the best, second only to running as a wolf. I love the power of the bike between my legs and the sheer speed. Fucking awesome. But no matter how fast I ride, there's no outriding the truth.

I love Keelie Sue and that means I have to set her free.

KEELIE SUE

I hear Jace before I see him. The roar of the bike's pipes bounce off the houses, filling my ears and making it impossible to concentrate on anything but the coming showdown. Jace called a pack meeting for this morning—and I didn't go. Honestly, I'm not sure the female pack members were invited, but even so... I should have been there. Standing by his side, nodding in approval and generally letting the other wolves know that things would be fine because we had a new Alpha and I was behind him one hundred percent. Instead I chickened out and stayed home.

I'm not sure things are fine at all.

He kills the bike and swings his leg over the seat,

one big, black boot hitting the pavement. The expression on his face is fierce and forbidding, which is my first clue he noticed my absence earlier. He strides toward my front door, and for a moment, I think he'll just push inside—I left the door unlocked because I don't want to push him too far—but then he slams a hand against the wood. I guess that's his version of a knock, and it's as good as I get today.

I hustle my ass to the door. When I open it, I'm eye-to-chest with Jace's leather jacket, the scent of leather and male flooding my senses. I catch traces of motor oil and something rougher and woodsier. *Jace.*

Carefully I tilt my head exposing my throat.

He curses, his fingers tightening on the doorframe. Not a good sign. "Can I come in?"

He's asking, not telling, but I hesitate and of course he notices. He makes me nervous, and I don't trust him, not entirely. He's big and now he's in charge, and... why *wouldn't* that be a problem for me? I step back, turn around, and head for my kitchen where Houdini is exploring the countertop, his little paw poking at the contents of my fruit bowl.

Jace eyes the kitten. "You kept one?"

Not the question I expected.

"Two," I admit, scooping up the kitten. Houdini needs company, after all.

"Soft touch." I can't tell if Jace's words are a tease, a complaint, or just a statement of fact.

"Got something to tell you," he adds with a sigh. He drags a kitchen chair out and swings himself onto the seat. Folding his arms on the back of the chair, he faces me. "You didn't come out to the clubhouse this morning."

As he tips the chair forward, I frown, trying to decide if I should make a break for it. But I'm done running. I came to that conclusion last night, when I'd been mentally debating his "invitation" to the clubhouse for a pack meeting. I took a pass, and instead I get the Alpha himself on my front porch. He's going to insist I talk to him.

"I didn't," I agree and wait to hear what he says next.

"And that means I've got a problem," he announces.

Welcome to the pack, right? I cradle the kitten closer to my chest.

He levels a hard look at me. "You want to hear what it is?"

"Do I have a choice?" I mutter the question, but he clearly catches it.

"Why can't you trust me?" he growls. "I've looked out for you. I've had your back. Hell, I got Big Red off you."

"You're the Alpha now!" I shout, my gaze flying up to meet his. Screw being submissive. Right now? Angry suits me just fine. "Big Red was a terrible dad, and his attitude was downright medieval. I get that he was no prize, but how can I trust that you'll be any different? Why would I *want* to stick it out with the pack after the crap that's happened to me there? Big Red mated me when I was sixteen! Do you have any idea what that was like?"

"Not a fucking clue," he roars back at me. His fingers tighten so hard on the back of the chair that I think the wood might snap. The kitten explodes from my arms in a flurry of squeaks and retreats down the hall. Lucky beast. "I did my best. I get that it wasn't good enough. That *I* wasn't good enough. But I'm learning, Keelie Sue. It's not like there's a manual for how to be an Alpha. I'm gonna fuck it up again, I shit you not."

"You didn't *ask* me whether I wanted to be your mate!" I holler the words at him, loud enough to be heard out on the street. "You have a tongue in your head. You could have asked. You knew Big Red didn't ask me, and you didn't bother to either. That was your choice."

Jace shoves off the chair and stalks toward me. Before I can take more than one sidelong step toward the door, however, he stops and slams his palm against my cabinet door.

"I fucked up."

Wait. Rewind. What?

He picks me up in his arms and swings me up onto the counter. Bracing his arms on either side of me, he leans his forehead against mine. It feels only too natural for me to wrap my legs around his lean hips and hug him tight. Heat sparks in me, a sweet, sexy blaze. My body has no problem acknowledging his dominance.

"You want to say that again?" I ask cautiously.

"Not at all." The grin he gives me is both rueful and endearingly cute.

Oookay. I blink at him. Stupid, silly thing to do, but he's surprised me, and suddenly I don't want to fly out the door.

"You're right," he continues. "I should have asked. But I'd never met someone like you before, someone who mattered. I didn't know what to say to you, or how to tell you that you made me want to be the best fucking Alpha ever, and that I needed you to do this with me. I saw a chance, and I took it. Would probably do it again too, so you're right to kick my ass to the curb because you don't trust me."

I don't know what to say to that. I truly don't. The sound of my heart pounding in my ears deafens me as I suck in air. Then right when I think he's going to kiss me—and that I won't mind one bit—he shoves away and my legs close on nothing.

"I came over here to give you this," he says. He picks up my hand and turns it over, smoothing out the fist I made until my fingers are straight and flat. He pulls an envelope out of his jacket and places it on my palm. Closes my fingers over it.

"Car keys," he announces. "Five thousand bucks. And a lease on a place in downtown Baton Rouge. One of those new condo places they just finished. It has good security, and you've got the top floor, so you just gotta remember to lock your door at night. You can move in today."

I gape at him. Sex, spanking games, yelling—those I expected. This is something else entirely. "Jace…"

"You wanted to be independent of the pack. You've got it."

I'm out of the pack? Home free and independent?

"What about—"

"Us?" He steps back. "Nothing you need to worry about. You didn't accept my mate claim. I'm a big boy, Keelie Sue, and contrary to what you think, I understand the word *no*. You're free."

And then he turns around and leaves.

## JACE

I SPEND THE NEXT week taking out the trash. Would be easier if I could shove the offending wolves inside a Hefty bag, but I have to deal with them in public. Not my first choice, not with the whole wolf pack watching to see how I handle shit, but I'm Alpha now.

Should be thinking about my next steps, but Keelie Sue keeps popping into my head and hanging out there like she has the right to remain. She doesn't have rights to me, I remind myself. Not after she rejected my mating claim and chose to walk.

Keelie Sue isn't mine.

The sooner I get that through my head, the better.

"You ready to ride?" Ware falls in beside me. The older wolf has spent the better part of the week sticking to me tighter than a cop on a felon.

"I should be asking you that." He's decided to hold

a private audition for the role of Alpha, and I'm about ready to kick his ass.

Ware rolls his shoulders, working the muscles. I can take him in a fight, but he'll make me work for it and I don't want to kill him. As soon as I'm sure of his loyalty, I'm making him my second.

He thinks a moment. Too fucking long. My body instinctively relaxes into a fighting stance, ready to take him down if he launches himself at me.

"I'm ready," he decides finally.

"Make up your fucking mind," I growl.

"I'm in." He spits the words out. Doesn't look happy, but I don't care. Much. "Who are we doing today?"

I hit the door, gunning for my bike. Ware follows close on my ass. "Big Dog," I grunt. I don't know the story behind the wolf's name, but right now I don't give two fucks. What I *have* heard, I don't like. Big Dog is a mean son-of-a-bitch, and he tends to believe rules don't apply to him.

I straddle my bike and turn to look at Ware in the ensuing pause. He knows where to find my target—the question is whether or not he gives up the other wolf. Big Dog took a mate six months ago—wolf-style. Gal didn't get a ring, a wedding, or even a Target registry. From what I've been able to learn, his woman isn't happy with the deal, starting with the lack of asking on Big Dog's part and ending with the wolf himself. I'm about to introduce her to divorce court, wolf-style.

"Tell me what you know about him." I stare Ware in the eye. The wolf needs to learn who's in charge here—and it's not him.

Fucker doesn't drop his gaze, but he does answer. "Big Dog was a lone wolf until about two years ago. Then Big Red patched him into the Breed. He likes fast bikes, shooting, and he's got a hunting cabin out in the bayou. We should start there. He keeps his girls there."

133

"He's got more than one?" I fire up my bike and head toward the street.

Ware follows, his front tire practically kissing my ass. "He did."

Ware doesn't provide any details, but I can fill in those blanks. The wolf on today's meet-and-greet list plays the field, taking what and who he wants. That's over. The wolves of the Breed will never be nice—not what I fucking want anyhow—but we'll play by *some* rules. Any wolf who sticks his dick where he's not invited is out of the pack.

Permanently.

Ware shouts a few directions my way, and then we ride in silence. The road peels away beneath my tires, a slick, dark ribbon of asphalt. Once we get out of the city, it's just us, the road, and the bayou. Ware takes point, since he's been out to Big Dog's place. Riding shotgun isn't my first choice, but it gets us there quicker, so good enough.

Big Dog's place is no palace. The rundown cabin sits on the edge of the bayou, close enough I'd bet flooding is a constant risk. The porch lists worse than a drunk at closing time, and Big Dog clearly spends zero time on home maintenance. I'd bet his place gets wet when it rains, and he's used the front yard as his personal dumpster. Real scenic. Bike parts, beer cans, and random bags of trash pepper the yard between the house and the road. I'll actually be doing the parish a favor if I toss a match on my way out.

I'm off my bike and halfway to the door before Ware kills his engine. Don't bother knocking, either. I'm not here to play nice.

The idiot inside is sloppy. Even if he hadn't been a raping son-of-a-bitch, I'd want him out of my pack. If he can't keep his place and his woman safe, I won't trust him with my wolves. He shoves to his feet when I bust through his front door, but he stops when he gets a good look at my face.

"We've got a problem," I tell him, and Big Dog nods, clearly mistaking the calm in my voice for approval or some such shit.

"Tell me what you need from me," he says eagerly. Fuck, but he's a people pleaser.

Guess he thinks he smells a promotion headed his way. Too bad for that cocksucker. I surge forward, planting my fist in the bastard's nose. Bull's eye. He falls back with a roar of pain.

"What the—" Two words too many as far as I'm concerned. As soon as I stepped inside, I smelled the female's pain and terror. I might not be able to see her, but her distress is one hundred percent clear. I drive my fist into Big Dog's stomach as hard as I can. A real nice crack follows the meaty sound of my knuckles planting themselves in his skin. Big Dog howls and drops to the floor.

"I'm gonna tell you about my problem." In case he gets any ideas about bowing out on our conversation, I plant my boot in the middle of his chest and lean down. Ware moves behind me, and I keep half an eye on him. That wolf is the real wild card in the room.

Big Dog snarls something uncomplimentary, and jackknifes, trying to throw off my hold. I shove down, something new cracks in the vicinity of the wolf's ribcage, and he finally shuts up, although that may be because breathing now presents a challenge. Good. We have shit to get straight.

"I'm in charge of this pack," I tell him. I wait until he whines out something close enough to agreement, press down a little harder, and get to the point of today's little visit. "And I told you boys that we've got a new rule. We don't rape our females. We don't put our dicks where we're not wanted—and if you're not man enough to get it right in bed, you don't get to force your way in there. Are we clear?"

Big Dog reaches for my boot, and I've had enough. Doesn't take much to snap both his arms so the fucker has to let go. When he's whimpering and bitching, I give him my nice smile.

"Why don't you tell us where you put your mate? Think of this as a welfare check. We're practically fucking social services. If she's happy, you're happy, and we go on our way."

"Fuck—" Big Dog starts, and that isn't the way this conversation is going. I kick him in the jaw, and while he's cursing and howling, I nod to Ware.

"Get her." Maybe this mating is a happy pairing and Big Dog is just having a bad day, but I don't think so. Ware must agree with me, because he follows his nose and makes straight for the closed door on the other side of the room.

Big Dog whines and curses, twisting as I do some more redecorating with my fists. There's a muffled curse from the bedroom, followed by a feminine whimper. Guess my instincts were dead-on right.

"You need help?" I land another blow on Big Dog's midsection, just to give myself something to do.

Ware comes to the door. He's shucked his jacket and his T-shirt, and I'm not gonna ask why. I have to start trusting my boys, and the look he levels on Big Dog says that right now Ware is all mine.

"I'm gonna kill him," Ware states his new plan matter-of-factly, starting forward.

Honestly? I agree with him. The human justice system can't hold a wolf, and the pack has its laws. Big Dog gets to die today, but I'm gonna be the judge and executioner. As Alpha, it's my job. Not Ware's. We'll sort that minor disagreement out in a moment.

"It bad?" I grab one of Big Dog's arms and Ware grabs the other. Working as a team, we drag the sorry son-of-a-bitch outside and toward the water. Looks like we've finally found common ground. Execute a few more wolves and maybe we'll even become besties.

"Bad enough," Ware grunts.

"She need a doctor?" We don't have one, but I'll figure it out.

"Not sure," he admits. "I'll get her back to Baton Rouge and see what she needs."

I drop my half of our werewolf load by the water's edge. "Not your place. Whatever she needs, I'll make sure she gets. We clear on that?"

Ware's boot lands on Big Dog's ribs. Good thing I intended to kill the bastard, because Ware proceeds to methodically crack the wolf's ribs like he's ripping open a crab leg. I half-expect him to shift and use his teeth to pick out the meat.

"Enough," I announce finally, because while Big Dog deserves the beat down, we have something— someone—else to take care of and dragging Big Dog's death out isn't helping her. If she catches sight of us working over her "mate," we'll probably scare her half to death. And if she runs from us, I'll have to chase her down. I'm not the most sensitive of guys, but even I know that's a bad idea.

Ware draws back with a curse, but he does it. Big Dog looks like shit. We've cracked his ribs. One eye is swelling shut, and blood trickles from his mouth. He'll heal quickly, though, so it's time to finish this.

"You broke pack law," I tell him, nudging his chin up with the tip my boot so his good eye meets mine. "Now I'm gonna have to kill you."

I don't bother shifting all the way—just let my wolf into my head, feeling my jaw reform and my canines grow. Then I tear out Big Dog's throat and we roll the stupid, raping bastard into the bayou. As the body sinks into the dark water, Ware nods like he's come to some kind of conclusion.

"I want to claim her," he announces. Didn't expect that.

"Big Dog's female?" It's not like the bayou is sprouting females, but I need to be clear.

"Yeah," he growls, already heading back to the cabin.

Fuck. I fall in behind him. Big Dog's female stands in the middle of the living room when we push our way back inside. I'm pretty sure she was fixing to run, which is a problem. She's barefoot. Hell, she appears to be naked except for Ware's T-shirt and jacket. Guess he found her in a bad situation and did his best to fix it. Bruises mottle her legs and arms, making me want to drag Big Dog out of the bayou and kill him all over again.

She squeaks when she spots us, but she also raises the two-by-four slat she must have pried out of the bed frame. Kind of like she's playing baseball and we're the ball.

"I'm leaving," she whispers hoarsely, her eyes darting to the open space behind us. She can look for Big Dog all she needs, but her bastard mate isn't coming back and the news seems more likely to inspire an hallelujah chorus than any regrets on her part.

"We'll give you a ride," I tell her. "You can ride with Ware or with me. You pick."

She hesitates, but it's not like I can order a fucking taxi to come and get her, not without raising questions the pack can't afford. Big Dog had a bike and a truck, but I'm not sure she should be driving. The makeshift bat in her hands shakes like hurricane-force winds are rocking the cabin. Let her take the wheel, and she'll end up in a ditch or the bayou.

"You got a name, honey?" Ware doesn't move from his position slouched against the wall, his hands loose on his thighs. I can smell the anger and tension radiating from him, but she isn't a wolf and maybe she'll buy it.

"Marly." Her voice is stronger this time.

"You got stuff you want to take with you, Marly?" I

reach in my pocket and fish out a lighter. This place leaves a bad taste in my mouth. Her eyes follow my hand, lasering in on the lighter. She sucks in a breath and freezes. Shit. I give her a body another quick once over, but spot no burn marks. Doesn't mean they're not there, though. "If so, you might want to grab it," I suggest.

She gives a small nod and disappears into the bedroom fast enough to suggest anyplace without wolves is the better choice. Yeah. We'll have to do something for her.

"There another way out?" I ask Ware. If Marly tears through the bayou barefoot and mostly naked, she'll do some serious damage to herself.

He shakes his head. "The windows in the bedroom are boarded up."

And... fuck.

"Not gonna fix that girl overnight," I tell him slowly. "If you're serious about claiming her, you're gonna have to wait. Some stuff takes time."

I'm no psychologist, but even I know Marly's gonna have the kind of damage you don't see.

Ware growls low in his throat. "You figure this out with Keelie Sue? Did you give her the time she needed?"

I spot the tension in his body, and the need. For some reason, Marly gets him going and he's chosen her. It doesn't have to make sense to me, but I do need to hear a *yes* from her before I hand her over to my boy. If she doesn't choose him, he doesn't get her. It's that fucking simple.

Of course, maybe that's where I'd fucked up with Keelie Sue now that I'm thinking with my big head and there's some space between us. I pushed, instead of giving her time. I wanted insta-trust from her, when she needed time to heal or to figure stuff out. Hell, maybe she just needed time alone. I didn't given it to her, though, and it had been my job to make sure she had what she needed.

She hadn't failed me—*I'd* failed *her.*

Marly sidles back out into the living room while I'm still working through this unpleasant revelation, her gaze darting between the two of us and fixating on the door. She definitely isn't ready to trust.

"You ready to ride?" I ask her. "You pick which one of us you want to ride with, and we'll get you somewhere safe."

She nods—which makes me want to take a victory lap—then her gaze returns to the lighter in my hand. I hold it out to her.

"You want to do the honors, honey?"

## KEELIE SUE

Life doesn't come with a gift receipt. I should write that on a Post-It note and slap it on my new fridge. I yearned to be free of the pack, and I got my wish and then some. I have a new place and enough money in the bank to hold me over while I figure out my next steps. Find myself a new, pack-free job, go back to school, take a cruise and blow it all on the slots as soon as I hit international waters… for the first time in my life, I have options.

I've put out some feelers job-wise, and I have an interview scheduled for next week. Things are just falling into place for me, and I should be doing a happy, happy dance each night when I go to bed. I've got it all. Sure my head swivels like I'm starring in *The Exorcist* whenever I hear a bike's pipes roar, but that's a minor detail. It's just because it seems too good to be true that I'm pack-free.

After two weeks, it seems kind of lonely.

Jace didn't ban me from talking to anyone in the pack, but I figure it was implied. If I want to walk away from all things wolf, I can't pop back for a chat or to go out for drinks, and it's not like I made any friends in the pack anyhow. The bikers are all guys—women aren't allowed to patch in and become members—and I never had a real opportunity to become friends with the women my father's wolves mated. Eventually, I know, I'll make human friends. We'll do human shit, and I'll build myself a new, human life.

*Eventually* doesn't mean *right fucking now* however, so alone it is for the foreseeable future.

I curl up on my new couch and consider my Sunday fun day options. I have a stack of paperbacks, a loaded Kindle, and a laptop. The building is quiet—most if not all of my new neighbors are still asleep because normal people don't wake up at dark o'clock on a weekend unless they have stuff to do. I don't have their commitments, and my wolf whines a little. I've ignored her the best I can, and she's lonely. Not sure what I thought would happen after I left the pack, but I've been kind of pretending to myself that I'm every bit as human as the other bodies in the building. I'm not good at lying, not even to myself.

I drag on my running shoes, pocket my keys, and let myself out. It's still early, the sun just threatening to poke over the horizon, and darkness blankets my neighborhood. I get into my new car and drive until I'm out of the city and it's just me, the road, and the bayou. When I roll down the window, the familiar scents pour in. Before I know it, I've pulled off onto the side of the road and killed the engine. Maybe a run can fix my all-over-the-map emotions.

I haven't shifted in months, but suddenly I can't wait. Getting out of my car, I take a quick look around, but the road is as empty and lonely as it was a minute ago. Okay then. Before I can overthink things, I strip, folding my clothes and dropping them onto the seat. When I'm naked, my bare toes curling into the dirt, I lock up, hide the car keys in some nearby bushes, and shift.

I never liked shifting, never welcomed the sickening sensation of my body rearranging itself to make room for my wolf, but today it feels more right than wrong. Kind of like stretching when you've sat too long, or working a painful kink out of a muscle. I just let go, and my wolf leaps to fill the empty spot inside me, yipping with pleasure when I stand there on four paws. I lift my head. Inhale.

*This* is *better.*

I don't have anywhere in particular to be or to go, so I just run, letting my wolf pick the direction. The sun comes up, flooding the bayou with light and warmth, the bright light bouncing off the water's smooth surface in almost painful slivers. The birds wake up too, calling to each other as they get on with the business of nesting and hunting down breakfast.

I've been running about an hour when I encounter the other wolf. His scent wraps around me, the smell both comforting and welcome, like life just set a hot stack of pancakes in front of me and I'm starving. My wolf drinks him in greedily, inhaling the masculine goodness of Jace's scent, and if I'd been in human form, I'd have had a big, dumb-ass grin painted all over my face. There are advantages to being a werewolf after all.

I'm upwind, and the big, dark wolf that lopes out of the bushes must not realize I'm there, because it freezes, its body radiating aggression. It only takes him a second to recognize me, the aggression changing into something else. His ears stand up and he stiffens his legs, radiating dominance.

Instinctively, I drop to the ground, rolling onto my back and watching Jace. My wolf whines happily, glad to see him and there isn't much the human part of me can do at the moment. Not like shifting's an option—a ten-mile naked hike through the bayou isn't anyone's idea of a good time.

Jace pads closer, standing over me. His nose nudges my throat, demanding a submission my wolf is only too happy to give him. The pleasure of that simple touch pools in my belly, shooting through my body like all of my nerves have formed a conga line and are dancing out their happiness at his nearness.

He *whuffs*, his breath teasing my ear, and I answer with a low yip of my own. I've come out here looking for something—a run, an escape—but maybe my wolf has a few plans of her own as well. He nudges, and I roll to my feet. I want to run all night. *With* Jace.

My wolf isn't interested in introspection. When Jace lopes toward the trees, I follow. We run for the better part of an hour. He leads, I follow, and I fall into the easy rhythm of his pace. He knows what I like, and I happily let him pick our path. I could turn, could have run in another direction or stop altogether, but both the wolf and I are unexpectedly happy.

Eventually he leads me back to my car. I don't know if he saw me arrive, if he watched me, or if he simply picked up my original trail and doubled back. I'm kind of sorry to see my car, but I'm also tired and there's a message in Jace's choice of destinations.

I shift by the edge of the road, where the trees provide more than enough cover in case we have unseen, unexpected human company. The wolf isn't worried about getting naked in front of Jace, so I go with it. The wolf's eyes bore into me as I snag my keys from their hiding place with trembling fingers, unlock the car, and pull on my clothes. He doesn't approach, just stands there and watches over me. That's what Jace

143

does, I realize. He keeps me safe. Instead of feeling stifled, I feel free. I can do what I need to do, and he'll have my back. He'll be watching so nothing bad happens while I go about my life—or he *has* been.

I told him we were done, and I walked away. Maybe I was stifling the wrong part of myself, though. Maybe my wolf needs to run and that's okay. Before I can say any of this, however, Jace turns and disappears into the trees.

Game over.

I think about him as I drive back to my new place, and then I think about the way things ended between us. My new place isn't bad, and in time I'll make it truly mine. But Jace doesn't fit here. He belongs out there in the bayou, running wild and free, and he belongs with my father's pack.

*Jace's* pack. He took care of his wolves, and he took care of me. Even after I rejected his help and betrayed his trust, he still made sure I got what I needed. He's not Big Red and if I believe that—truly believe that—then I've kicked the best man, the best wolf I'll ever meet to the curb. He might be possessive, but I'm not just a possession to him. When he looks at me, he sees Keelie Sue, and he cares for her. I've made him pay for Big Red's mistakes and for my own, when I should have wrapped both arms around him and hung on. My wolf whines in agreement, sorry that Jace has left us in the bayou, and for the first time she and I are in complete agreement.

"I'll fix it," I promise her and the empty condo. Trying feels like finding the right trail through the bayou, a trail that might or might not lead back to Jace, but that I need to take.

Grabbing my laptop, I look up the nearest Harley-Davidson showroom. A Harley won't be the same as a custom ride, but I have a point to make—and I want to make it now.

# 10

JACE

I STOPPED BY THE CLUBHOUSE to work on my bike. Something somewhere was leaking oil, and Saturday afternoon is as good a time as any to strip it down and see if I can find the problem. I'm not the only wolf playing mechanic, either. Both Fang and Ware have their tools out, pieces of their bikes strewn around them. If a cop drives by, we'll probably look like we've gone into the chop shop business.

The roar of pipes bouncing off the building walls has my head swinging around. Don't know what makes me look up, but holy shit. The bling on the bike headed toward me is downright blinding. It's a big, black Harley with a shiny paint job with… pink sequins on the pedals. Along with a stiletto boot.

Hello.

That boot is hand-job material, and as I drag my

145

gaze up the boot's owner, I can't decide which is better—the black leather pants cupping a very nice pair of legs, the formfitting jacket, or the naughty pair of lips smiling my way. I know that mouth.

"Keelie Sue." I shove to my feet and wipe my greasy hands on a bandana. This is either really good or really bad. Since I've set her free from the pack, she has no business riding up to our front door.

No matter how hot she looks doing it.

She kills the bike, straddling the seat as she pulls off the helmet and shakes her hair free.

"New hobby?" I nod my head toward her bike, trying not to devour her with my eyes. I wasn't good enough for her, and that is my problem. I'll fucking respect her now though.

She bites her lip, but she keeps her gaze pinned on mine. Christ. I want to lick her mouth, shove my tongue inside and kiss her hello. "I've come for what's mine."

"Oh, yeah?" I toss the rag on the ground. "You didn't clean the place out when you left?"

A responsible Alpha doesn't wrestle a female wolf to the ground and show her with his body exactly how much he's missed her. Turning over a new leaf sucks.

She looks kinda mutinous. "You're the one who told me to go."

"You made it clear you didn't want to stay," I counter. Fuck. I've heard wolf pups marshal better arguments than that crap. "What did you leave behind?"

"You." She throws a leg over the bike, and fucking hell, she doesn't hesitate. She eats up the pavement in those boots and makes straight for me. I open my arms up when she gets close because otherwise she'd slam into me and I've kinda missed her.

More than missed her.

Fuck, I've been hers since day one, and if she's come back, that works for me.

## KEELIE SUE

Jace opens his arms and I walk into them, ignoring the eyes of the other wolves on us.

"I claim you." Jace's hard eyes soften when he looks at me, and I don't think it's because he's remembering me naked as a jaybird in his bed.

"Right back at you," I declare fiercely. I'm done waiting for crap to happen to me. If Jace takes me, I take him.

"It won't be easy." He rubs my shoulder with his hand, his thumb drawing a seductive back and forth motion on my skin. "You want easy, you gotta stay away from the pack."

"I tried it. I didn't like it," I admit.

"That's over. You're pack." His arms tighten around me, and I have a feeling that he won't ever let go if he thinks I'm really headed for the proverbial door.

Running isn't the answer anymore either. Some memories stick with a girl. Jace is one of those, but in a good way. I don't want to forget him.

*He* is pack. My previous role in the Breed was downright humiliating. I was their accountant, their punching bag, and their sometime whore. I'm never going there again.

"*My* pack," Jace clarifies, like he knows exactly where my head went. "You're always first."

I like that. I've never been first before.

He lowers his head and brushes his mouth over mine, softlike. "You got feelings for me, sweetheart."

"I've got something." I see his face so close to mine, his eyes filled with the *something* I've craved for so long without knowing it. Jace Jones is my Alpha, my wolf, and my everything.

His thumb dips lower, trailing over the sensitive skin at the juncture of my arm. "And I've got something for you."

He steps away from me for a moment, snagging something from the saddlebag on his bike. Leather rustles, then he returns, holding a small black box. He sets the box in my palm, curling my fingers around it.

"I thought we could do this thing both ways, human and wolf, but there's a couple of things you should know before you open that. First, I claimed you, my wolf claimed you. If you've got any doubts on that account, I'm happy to settle them."

He's called me his before, and that time he marked me with his scent and with his body. He's so right that I ache with the knowledge. He set me free, but what I want—*who* I want—is standing right here in front of me, and I'll take whatever he offers me.

"Second, I love you. Should have said that sooner, but we had shit to work out, and the moment wasn't right. So I'm saying it now. You can say it back or not, but you gotta be honest with me. You say yes and you put that on, you don't run from me again."

"Because I've used up my chances?" I turn the box over in my hand.

"Because you'll fucking break my heart, Keelie girl."

That's my cue to open the box and my breath catches. The ring, nestled in a little bed of black velvet, blazes with diamonds surrounded by tawny-colored stones. Topaz.

"Reminded me of you," he says. "Pretty but hard as nails when someone tries to beat on you. And you've got gorgeous wolf eyes."

"You think we can work this out?"

"Not gonna be easy," he acknowledges. "Pretty sure I'm gonna keep on giving orders and you'll get pissed off sometimes, but yeah... I think we can work it out."

"You really mean it?" I reach up and tug his face down to mine. "About loving me?"

"Every word," he says hoarsely. "You wanna put me out of my misery here?"

"I love you," I tell him, sliding my hands up his arms and linking them behind his head. Doesn't mean I don't still have questions though. And honestly, I'm not sure what kind of relationship we can have moving forward. He's the new Alpha of the Breed, and I've spent a lifetime wanting to put as much distance as possible between me and the wolves. Accepting Jace's mating claim means I don't ever walk away from the pack.

He kisses me then, the world narrowing to the man who holds me in his arms so carefully. Jace might be rough on the outside, but on the inside he's all mine. He kisses me. I kiss him back because I'm not doing this thing halfway, and it's a long time before either of us comes up for air. When we do, though, I still have one question.

"Are we okay now?" I rejected him and then walked away from him, after all, and wolves aren't the forgive-and-forget type.

He catches my lower lip with his teeth and nips lightly. "We're good. At least you didn't try to feed me to the gators like your first mate."

I'm never living that down, so I punch him in the arm. Jace just laughs and settles me closer. He's won this round, and we both know it. Still, things are changing too fast, and my head kind of swims when I think about it all. Less than a week ago, Jace was a sexy memory (or a darned embarrassing one, depending on how I took that spanking). Now we're mates, and he leads my pack. It's like my life jumped on a roller-coaster and I scored a lifetime of free rides. It's all good—but I really want a chance to calm down.

"Can we slow things down just a little?"

He looks down at my hand, which has somehow found its way to his chest. My fingers draw little circles on his shirt, tracing a naughty pattern around his nipple through the fabric. "Give me more words."

"Date. Try normal things and get to know each other." I shrug.

He stills. "You don't want this?"

By *this*, he means *himself*, and no, that isn't what I mean at all.

"I love you," I repeat, "but I want to take things slow. Figure out how we fit together when we're not in bed."

His slow smile is downright wicked. "You realize we can have sex somewhere other than a bed, right?"

That grin lights me up from the inside out—Jace smiles, and I melt. I have a feeling that's going to happen plenty more times. He's so gorgeous and he's all mine.

"You can play show and tell," I whisper to him, and his breath hitches, growing rougher.

"I want you to wear my ring," he says. "You want time, I'll give you time. I'll give you the fucking world if that's what you want, but the pack needs to understand that we're together."

"Okay," I agree, looking down at the box in the hand that isn't groping Jace. "I can do that." It isn't like we aren't already married in the eyes of the pack. Shoot, according to wolf law, he owns me body and soul. It doesn't change how we feel about each other, but it's a big part of what makes me want to feel my way a little more slowly into this relationship.

"And I want you to move in with me."

I eye him suspiciously. "Which part of *slow things down a little* did you not understand?"

He gives me that naughty choirboy smile of his, the one guaranteed to melt my panties. "I'm not balls-deep inside you, Keelie Sue. That's about as slow as you're getting."

Point taken.

"I'm not okay with leaving you on your own," he continues. "Big Red put you up for grabs, and then I challenged and won. I don't want any loose cannons thinking they can grab you and make a play for leadership."

We both turn and look at Fang. That wolf is going to cause problems. Ware, the other wolf in the garage, must agree, because he shoves to his feet and starts herding Fang out of there. Fang lets him, too. That's almost as surprising as the fact that Jace doesn't push. He just waits for me to think things through and decide. I get the feeling that he's willing to wait as long as it takes—two minutes, two hours, two years.

Okay, so not two years, and the two hours is also in question. I guess I have to give him credit for trying—he hasn't issued an order. "You in?"

Question. Not command.

He's practically housebroken right there. *Not.* I can't hold back my snort. Life with Jace will never be easy.

He holds out his hand to me, and waggles his fingers. I have no idea how I'm supposed to resist that particular invitation, because the man looks damned fine. His jeans hang low on his hips, his jaw rough with stubble. I look down at the ring box in my own hand.

"You've got me," he says, low and rough. "Ring or no ring, mate or not, I'm all yours, and that's the fucking truth. If I could, I'd tattoo it on my heart. I'm gonna get things wrong between us sometimes, but you're gonna be the one who puts me right. It scares the shit out of me sometimes, how much you mean to me. Can't imagine life without you and yeah, that makes me want to lock you up somewhere safe. We can take this as slow as you want, but I need you to know that."

His words shock me, warm me, melt me…

I pop the ring out of its velvet bed and slide it on my finger. Things aren't over between us—we're just getting started.

"I love you," I say, because I can't say it too many times, and then I put my hand in his.

## 11

KEELIE SUE

APPARENTLY I MAKE A habit of falling asleep after good sex. Hours after I rode up to Jace and told him I loved him, I wake up hours later in his bed, my wolf wrapped around me. He's buried his face in my hair, his mouth resting against my throat, and I relax into the steady sound of his breathing. And when I test my need to get up and run, to put this man behind me? I get nothing. I've done my running, and he's caught me. He's nothing like my dad, and I trust him.

I really, really trust him.

"I can hear you thinking," he growls against my ear, startling a squeal out of me. "If you're awake, you've got two choices."

The way his dick presses up against my butt, iron hard, I'm pretty sure I know my first choice. He spanked me once, and then he promised to take my ass. He told me he'd fill me up every way he could, and I've never shaken the erotic brutality of his words.

Not only do I want Jace, but I want him every way possible. And he… wants to be my Alpha, in bed and out. We've covered what happens outside our bedroom, but I've never let him take over in bed, not entirely. The desire filling me to let go completely is crazy. Am I really ready for that?

"We can talk," he says, voice low and rough, "or we can fuck. Probably can't do both at the same time, seeing how you get under my skin and drive me crazy."

Once he gets started, I'm not capable of much more than *yes* and *more, please*. I'm riding the crazy train with him. He nudges me onto my back and leans up on his elbow, studying my face carefully. He's sinfully gorgeous and all my reservations melt. I do trust him.

"Okay," I say.

He cups my jaw with one big hand, and he's both careful and rough, and I'm suddenly, immediately turned on. This is so right that the feelings are almost painful.

"You're gonna have to explain that one to me," he says.

"You're my Alpha," I tell him, and his mouth quirks up.

"You've got that right." He strokes his thumb over my bottom lip.

"I trust you. Whatever you want to do, I'll do it."

He stills and I relax into him, my body touching his. "Anything?"

He'd never hurt me. I know this. I don't need caveats or asterisks. "Anything," I promise him.

"Once I start, you tell me to stop if you need me to."

"I don't want you to stop." I roll onto my stomach and look over my shoulder at him. He looks fierce and predatory, all that masculine power focused on me. I'm really the one in control here, because he can't force my trust. Can't take it or make me give it up. It's a gift I want to give him. "You'll give me what I need, and I'm going to do the same for you."

His face radiates strength and a possessiveness that I can't, won't resist. The truth is, he *is* my Alpha—and I trust him. Whatever happens between us in bed is as much my giving him what he needs—and he needs my trust.

"You got it," he says, but all I need is him.

He pulls me up onto my knees. He's so much larger than me, and yet I've never felt more important. He presses up against me, molding me against his body, and heat surges through me. He smells so good, feels so close, and he's all mine. The desire radiating through me is wild and out of control, a liquid pulse between my thighs that screams *touch me*.

He reaches out and wraps my wrists in one hand. Then he guides my hands to the headboard even as he urges me back against him with his other hand. He's aroused, his erection long and thick against my butt, and maybe playing games wasn't my best idea because he's going to make me wait for it. Make me wait for *him*. "Don't let go," he orders and I nod.

There's so little space left between us, my body meeting his and filling up the emptiness. If I did let go, there wouldn't be far to fall at all. He's waiting for my answer though, poised against me and I hear my breath hitch in anticipation. I don't actually know what he will do if I let go, only that I'm going to enjoy every single second of it.

"I'll try," I promise him, not sure when my voice got so throaty. Those two words sound raw and needy, and I should probably be scared he can set me on fire so easily. Except I see the same need mirrored in his eyes.

"No," he growls, his mouth closing over my ear.

Heat spears through me. "Trying's not good enough. You're gonna do what I tell you. Every. Single. Thing. You're gonna trust me to take care of you."

And just like that I'm all *yes*.

He drags his belt up my legs. We'd slept naked, but he must have reached down and grabbed it from the floor where we'd dropped our clothes. The leather presses between my legs.

"Open," he commands and I slide my legs wider to accommodate him, drinking in the rough-smooth sensation of the leather slipping over my core. There's no hiding my arousal. For a moment I shift helplessly, off-balance, but he steadies me with a hand on my hip. I crave more, lifting to meet his touch, and he gives me everything. The leather presses against me harder, and each raw, rough stroke feeds my hunger for this man of mine.

"I'm gonna make you come a hundred different ways," he tells me and I jerk involuntarily as my brain supplies the images to match his words. He's dark and dangerous, and he's all *mine*.

When he drags the leather up my body and over my stomach, I moan. He knows just how to touch me, how to teach every inch of me that he's in charge here.

"Shhh." He nips my ear and I buck. I need him in me. *Now.*

He flips me around and ties me to the bed. It's like before, when Cruz interrupted us, but different. I can't stop staring at the belt looped around my wrists, stretching me out like some kind of virgin sacrifice, except there's nothing virginal about the way he makes me feel and I'm more than willing to be here with him. He pushes all my buttons in the best possible way.

"Jace—" I moan his name as I test my bonds. Not because I want to get away but because I *don't*. I want him to hold me here, keep me here. Forever absolutely works for me.

"You don't get to say *no* now," he warns me.

Big hands come down on either side of me, caging me between the bed and Jace's hard body. There's nowhere I'd rather be.

"But right now I want to get in here," he growls, pressing his thumb against my mouth. I bow to the pressure, opening up, and he presses in, my tongue tasting his skin. "Gonna fuck your mouth first."

I'm completely on board with that plan.

He tugs me downward and I go willing. God, he has a gorgeous dick. Not that he wants to hear that, but it's true and I'm definitely in a position to know. I spread my knees on the bed because I so do not want to fall over now, lean in, and drag my tongue up the thick, hard length of him.

I open my mouth and he guides himself home. Jace isn't a small man—my lips are stretched around his dick and I can feel the pull in my jaw already. He pushes in slowly, steadily, and I try to take all of him. He bumps against the back of my throat, and I tense. Breathing suddenly seems like an impossibility.

"Easy," he breathes roughly, his hands fisting in my ponytail.

He won't hurt me. If I need to stop, he'll pull away. Knowing that, I relax. I take more of him, swirling my tongue over the fat head. I've never had the chance to explore him before, and he tastes good. I lick and suck, learning every inch of him as he pushes into my mouth. Pulls out, then drives himself slowly back in. He fucks my mouth deliberately, but his fingers tighten in my hair, a subtle, wonderful, desperate message. He needs this. He needs *me*.

As I suck him, he whispers rough, hoarse commands. Telling me what to do, how to take him, how to make him feel the same pleasure he's given me. His hands pull my hair, slowing me down, speeding me up. He's in control of my motions, but it's my tongue

157

driving him wild and I love every moment, each brush of his dick against my mouth, my tongue, my lips.

I'm nowhere near ready to stop when he jerks away from me with a curse. He's always had lightning fast reflexes. He strokes his fingers down my folds, holding me open.

"You don't come, not until I tell you." He growls the command and it takes an act of will to obey when I can feel each rough word deep in my body.

Funny how hanging on tight is also a form of letting go. Because as Jace takes me higher, teasing my body until the pleasure makes me tighten almost painfully, I'm also free to let go.

# JACE

Keelie Sue isn't holding back, and it's the most fucking erotic thing I've ever seen. I could never deserve a woman like this, but she's picked me and I'm going to do everything I can to make her happy. Never knew that fucking a woman's mouth could be so hot, or maybe it's that trust in her pretty brown eyes. Doesn't matter because right now I need to make her come.

When I push my hand between her legs, she opens right up with a moan. She likes what I do to her, and she's not afraid to let me know it. She's flushed, her pussy the sweetest pink color I could lick from head to foot.

"You got any idea how pretty you are?"

She squeaks, and I grin against her pussy. Not gonna lie—I love the way she colors up and gets embarrassed. No one else gets to see her like this and I know I'm a lucky bastard.

"How about I show you?" I don't wait for an answer. I just sink my fingers into her wet heat and stroke. She's so soft on the outside, even though she's strong on the inside. Because I'm some kind of fucking gentleman and she's mine and this is all about her feeling good, I cradle her butt and her thighs with my palms. That way she's not going anywhere and I've got her right where I want her.

"Jace—" She moans my name, and it's like a twenty-four-gun salute going off in my heart.

"You're wet, sweetheart. This all for me?"

It had better be. If I screw this up, I lose my everything. That's stupid and poetic—and really fucking true. Since she gives a little moan as I push two fingers into her, I figure I'm doing my job right. She's as sweet and warm on the inside as she is on the outside. Keelie Sue is a giver, and I'll take everything she has to give me. I draw back, push inside deeper and harder as her eyes flutter closed.

"You made me wait two weeks for you. Did you miss me?"

Her eyes fly open. I drive my fingers inside her body, finding the sensitive spot that makes her push against me. I've thought about her constantly since she walked away from me, and I'm not above a little revenge right now.

"You want me to fuck you, Keelie Sue? Show you what you missed all those nights?"

Her fingers curl around the leather of my belt. So. Fucking. Gorgeous.

"Please," she whispers, and that one word? Better than all the poetry in the world. For whatever reason, I do it for her, and she's okay with that.

So I take care of her, because that's my promise to her. She's trusting me, and I'll always make it good for her. She's my goddess, my love, and dropping to my knees to worship her is easy. A quick tug and she's over me, riding my face. She makes a small, startled sound, part embarrassment, part pleasure, and I'm happy to convince her to give me a chance.

I lick her slowly, starting with her slit and working my way higher. She tastes so goddamn perfect. I get my fingers and my tongue to work showing her how good she feels.

When long minutes later I feel her pussy start to tighten, her thighs tensing, I give her a tiny smack right on her clit. She's squeezing my fingers tight and she's close. She squeals and I grin. We can both smell her arousal.

"Nuh-uh. Not yet."

She mutters something and I grin. Pretty sure she wasn't complimenting my pretty face. Christ, but I love this woman. "You don't come until I say so."

She gives me a look, which is difficult considering I'm planted between her thighs, but the frustration on her face is both cute and needy and I think she might gut me soon. I won't make her wait too long—my dick's so hard, it feels like it might crack.

"Yes," she says, and those three letters mean fucking everything to me. Better yet, she relaxes into my touch and that trust of hers about kills me.

"Watch me," I order, finding her clit with the pads of my fingers. "Keep your eyes on my face while you come for me."

I circle once, twice, and she keens.

"I can't," she pleads, and I'm not sure if she's begging to come or telling me this is all too much.

"I've got you," I growl, and then she can, because the tiny tremors grow stronger and I love that I can drive her crazy, that I can give her this. "Come for me now."

I tap her clit with my fingers and she gives me everything, coming with a shriek and holding nothing back.

She's still coming when I drive into her until I'm balls-deep, coming home, come with her. She's the one who submits in our relationship, but she's also the one with unbreakable hold on my heart. I love her with everything I am and nothing's fucking going to change that. I'll never be tamed and I'll always be her Alpha, but this wolf's heart is hers.

**Hide your virgins...AGAIN! The original Bad Boys are BACK and they're hotter than ever!**

These are not your mother's Vikings. Being a werewolf's mate sucks, but Bera doesn't have a choice—until a big, brutish, and thoroughly pissed-off Viking crashes into her cave and rescues her. He may be hot and their chemistry off-the-charts good, but she's done with domination games and alpha males.

Colden isn't a nice guy—and he likes it that way. His rules are simple. Hit hard, fight mean, and defend what's his. But when the Viking berserker rescues a sexy little werewolf and her pack names Colden as her new mate, the rules change. She wants to bargain for her freedom. He wants to keep her. Forever.

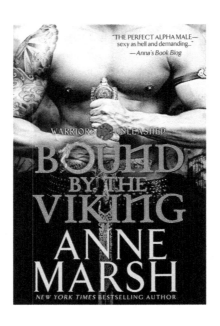

# Excerpt from Bound by the Viking

Freya's tits, but the wolf den was no Four Seasons. Even after I killed my snowmobile and strode inside the cave, the cold beat at me like Thor's hammer. The bitter scent of smoke and kerosene heaters didn't add to the ambiance, plus the mangy scent of werewolf was overwhelming. How the shifters managed to stink like wet fur and *eau de old dog* when it was ten degrees below zero out was a mystery, but that was winter in Greenland for you and reason number one why we Vikings had gone a-sailing all those centuries ago.

I slid a glance up at the ceiling. The caves were none too scenic, either. The decorating style consisted of dirt, rocks, and a shitload of ice and snow. If I'd been a werewolf, my vote would have been for tropical relocation ASAP.

Oh wait. Werewolves weren't democratic. They were an autocratic, rule-by-the-fist race, and the last werewolf Alpha had made the unilateral decision to relocate his pack to this particular armpit of Greenland in preparation for launching an attack on Odin. And yet looking at the sorry assortment of wolves lurking in the shadows, it got harder and harder to believe that the werewolf pack was actually a player in Ragnarök. These sorry ass pieces of fur were supposed to coordinate an assassination attempt on Odin, the ruler of the Norse gods? Not fucking likely.

I checked the ceiling again, but other than a new icicle or two, nothing. Nay. Pigs weren't flying yet.

Out of ideas, I elbowed my fellow Viking. "Remind me again why we're here."

Vars bared his teeth. Guess he didn't care for the poke. "Because Calder's bride convinced her shiny new husband that her pack planned on assassinating Odin, and since Calder's busy banging said new bride, someone else has to take point on investigative duty. You're an ugly bastard and I don't give a rat's ass, which makes up for my pretty face. That makes us perfect for the job. Or possibly the rest of our clan just wanted some alone time without us and decided we could manage Calder's pack while he's on honeymoon duty."

A hard punch to my gut accompanied this last.

I didn't give a damn about the blow. It took more than that to make me flinch, and we both knew it. Punches were merely punctuation in a conversation. I still didn't understand how our brother, Calder, had decided that not only would he take a mate, but he'd take a mate who came with an entire ready-made werewolf clan. Werewolves were not the ideal accessory, even for a Viking warrior who shapeshifted into a bear when he went berserk in battle. And if these werewolves had truly plotted to take down Odin, they were a liability because it would only be a matter of time before some other Norse god or goddess came gunning for them.

"We could just kill the wolves," I suggested. A quick takedown was neater and required none of this talking bullshit. Possibly, I'd made my suggestion too loud, because the nearest werewolf cringed away. *Loser.*

Vars didn't disagree. "Killing would be simpler, but Calder's mate is fond of her pack."

"*All* of the pack?" Every pack had a few assholes that could be sacrificed for the greater good.

Vars grinned. "You make an excellent point."

"We'd be in and out quicker too. You really want to spend the night here?" The cave did not improve upon closer acquaintance.

"You think it's an option to leave and check in somewhere cozier?" Vars held my gaze steadily as if leaving were really an option. "What are the odds these wolves act different if we're not around?"

Pretty good because from what I'd seen so far, pack life centered around fear and dominance. You ran scared—or you dominated. Since being afraid wasn't part of my vocabulary, that put me in Camp B. I planned on kicking just enough werewolf ass to discover what the pack alpha's plan for Ragnarök had been.

"If Leif wasn't talking shit, he had a plan. A weapon. A secret ninja stealth assassin."

"He had something," Vars agreed. "We just haven't found it yet. Hate to say it, but it may take us some time."

I lifted a shoulder because the man wasn't wrong. "I don't have anywhere else to be, but I would like to wrap this up before Calder finishes his honeymooning shit."

A knowing grin split Vars' face, making it all too obvious why my man here had his pick of the females. Me, on the other hand? I sported a scar down on one cheek, the earning of which had taken care of my pretty days. Which had probably lasted all of five minutes anyhow. Being not dead was far preferable to good looks.

"Best wedding present ever," Vars agreed. He moved deeper into the cave. Sleeping bags lined the walls, some of them laid out on blow-up air mattresses. Crap spilled from duffel bags and someone had invested in the full line of cheap-ass camping pots. I doubted the pizza delivery guy made it out here—or that the wolves had the cash to start with. I'd visited plusher digs in the Medieval Ages.

Calling the cave Spartan was an insult to the Greek fighters. Owning your own personal werewolf pack seemed more akin to paying through the nose for a property that the online copy touted as possessing "prime ocean views in the metropolitan center" but that turned out in reality to be a fixer-upper fishing shack on the middle of an ice floe in Antarctica. Or worse.

Because this cave and these werewolves definitely fell in the *worse* category. Somewhere deeper inside the cave a female whimpered in pain, the soft sound almost drowned out by a deeper, masculine growl.

Fuck. I hated it when females cried.

I should walk on. Get the ass-kicking over with, uncover the wolves' nefarious plans for Odin, and get back to my life. The message from my brain didn't reach my feet, however, which stopped dead. Yeah. I was going to have to do something about it.

I looked over at Vars. "Pit stop."

We'd already spent a good part of the day getting to the werewolf den, so Vars had to be itching to get on with our official business, but he simply nodded agreeably and fell in by my side, letting me take point. He was the kind of guy who, if I announced that I planned on doing some werewolf culling, would just ask me where he should start. He had my back, same as I had his.

Another whimper followed by a low growl. The female was down a passageway to my left. *She* wasn't the secret assassinate-Odin's-ass weapon. From the sound of things, she was on the bottom of the food chain in this cave, maybe literally.

Vars shot me a glance. "Rescue mission?

Fuck if I knew, but I guessed I wasn't getting back to the job until I'd made a few things clear to the ass-hole bothering the female. As of right now the cave was under new management. *My* management. While Calder chased down his mate—and fucked the living daylights out of her on a three-week honeymoon somewhere a hell of a lot warmer than Greenland—I'd been temporarily promoted. Alpha dead, long live the new Alpha and all that *shite*. Which meant Werewolf Asshole needed to learn some new manners.

The side room—side cave, whatever—was ten steps down the passageway. The place wasn't built for men my size, so I had to hunch over which kind of sucked. Vars whistled quietly behind me, his weapon making an almost inaudible snick as he pulled the blade from its sheath.

No point in knocking. It wasn't as if I planned on asking permission. I shoved aside the blue tarp covering the door. My personal theory was act first, think later, and right now a whole lot of unwelcome instincts pounded at me. *Unfamiliar* instincts like *protect* and *comfort.*

What. The. Fuck?

The werewolf was mostly naked, displaying far more werewolf skin than I needed to see. He'd pulled his belt from its loops, the better to smack the shit out of the female he'd pinned to the wall. That right there was reason number one why the wolf needed to die. The cocksucker had also unbuttoned his jeans partway, giving gave me a bonus peep show, and that was thing number two I hadn't needed to see. The precarious position of his jeans on his hips made it plenty obvious that the bastard was thoroughly enjoying the beat down he was administering.

In fact, the stupid bastard was so into his situation that he failed to hear us coming. I yanked him away from the female and sent him careening into the opposite wall. Conveniently he hit headfirst. Maybe the crack would knock some sense into him.

The female took one look at me and dropped to the floor, arms going up over her head.

"Next time, knee him in the balls," I said in the general direction of the brown hair covering her face. "And then run. Got me?"

She squeaked and I didn't think the sound was an affirmative. This was why my dating life sucked and my brothers had gotten all the strong, feisty women. Here I was, trying to make her feel better, and instead I'd only scared her worse. At least I hadn't gone berserk and shifted. That had to count for something.

Vars shoved his blade back into its sheath. "You're blocking the door, dumb ass. How's she supposed to get by you?"

The werewolf groaned. I'd have to make sure he hurt worse than he did, because the female sniffed. Quietly, like she was trying not to make too much noise.

Tears. Not my thing. Plus she acted like I roasted puppies for fun when all I'd tried to do was help her. This was the problem with good deeds. I should have borrowed a page from the Valkyries and squashed my Boy Scout urge in the bud. Hel, for all I knew, I'd interrupted some kind of kinky werewolf game.

Except... the cave smelled like fear. And she bit back another sob.

"You want me to kill him?" I asked her. Look at me, soliciting opinions and acting all open-minded. But I had to do something. Walking away now, leaving her broken on the floor, everything in me argued that was wrong and I'd spent a lifetime living by my instincts. Leaning down, I got my hand under her chin and nudged her face up. Silky, impossibly soft skin met my fingertips. *Ours* my bear roared inwardly. *This one is* ours.

Fuck. Was the werewolf mating urge contagious? She resisted my upward tug, hiding her face in her arm. She was curvy in my favorite places, her body softly rounded and downright sweet. Of course, I'd eat her for breakfast. The terrified message her body telegraphed said she knew it, too. I needed to get the hell out of this cave and get on with my life.

Whatever this *thing* was that I felt when I looked at her, it was temporary. A chemical thing or some kind of raw, beast-like attraction. I'd kill the male werewolf and stomp out of here; she'd live happily ever after or not, but at the opposite end of the world from me. I forced myself to let go while the silence stretched out between us and her tears dried up some. Somehow, leaving the cave didn't seem to be an option for me.

"I'm waiting for my answer." My gaze flicked over her, assessing the damage. Nothing too permanent, but she'd have bruises and that pissed me off. From what I could see of her, she was tiny. I'd bet her head would barely reach my chest if I could coax her off the ground. Her hair was all tangled up and I had the strangest urge to smooth the wild locks into place. The male werewolf had torn up her clothes, her T-shirt hanging off one shoulder, exposing a lacy pink bra strap I'd bet she'd die rather than show me. She wore a man's flannel shirt and nothing else, her bare feet curled into the cold floor.

The werewolf definitely needed to die.

"I'm taking silence as a *fuck yeah*," I told her. She started to say something, then hesitated. Girlie had more spine than I'd thought, however, because she eyed the crumpled pile of wolf like she might actually go all judge and jury on his sorry ass. Her ring finger was bare, although I had no idea if werewolves marked their territory with wedding bands, or if they were more the type to bite and piss all over things. Frankly, I was putting my money on the second option because living in a cave in Iceland screamed *uncivilized*.

Naturally, the werewolf picked that moment to groan and roll to his feet, proving all over again that he was ten different kinds of stupid. Done dealing with him and his shit, I slammed a fist into his jaw. Reacting beat the hell out of chitchatting.

"Nice," Var whistled. "Your management style is direct and forceful. I'm sure Calder will be properly appreciative when he returns from the honeymoon and only *some* of his wolves are broken."

The wolf female flinched and scooted backward, so naturally I turned straight back to her like a Viking homing pigeon. There was no reason for me to be so interested in her. I'd accomplished the rescue and now I was free and clear to leave. My bear rumbled a protest. Yeah. Maybe leaving wasn't on the day's agenda. I has a feeling though that I was looking at her like I had some brand-new Friday evening plans of my own.

"You got a name, sweetheart?" Var crouched, reaching for the female. Fuck If I knew what my brother was doing—his dating life had become nonexistence after he'd been the third in our leader's threesome—but I didn't want him touching the little werewolf and *that* was an unwelcome surprise. My bear got right on board with the possessiveness too, trying to shift right through my skin.

"Yeah," I growled, feeling my bear rise toward the surface. "Mine."

Fuck me, but he needed to rethink his *react first, think later* mission statement. Vars halted his forward momentum, shooting me a glance like he wanted to know what was up. Problem was, I had no idea.

"Mine," I repeated. Yeah. That was my voice making claims. Funny how the word still sounded right.

"Funny," Var rumbled and the bastard sounded like he was trying to keep his laughter at bay. "Is she the secret weapon?"

Ha ha.

The little wolf's back hit the wall, cutting off her escape route—hadn't I *told* her to run for the door, first chance she got?—and she tipped her head back. The curtain of brown hair fell back from her face, giving me a good look at the purple and yellow bruises decorating her left cheekbone—and the world kind of came to a standstill like I was starring in my very own greeting card commercial. One of those hokey ones where the lovesick bastard lopes across a flower-filled meadow pulling dance moves no self-respecting male would ever cop to, let alone with an audience. My bear hummed happily, clearly more in tune with his inner Hallmark than I was.

And now that I'd had a good look at her face, I realized that I knew this werewolf. She was considerably more dinged up and battered than the first and only time I'd seen her before, which made me see red all over again. Of course, she hadn't been in a good situation before either, but maybe I could fix things this time. I'd chosen to be the good guy that night and walk away from what had been offered to me, but here was Fate, dangling her in front of my nose again. I'd treat her better than the fucking werewolf, that was for certain.

"Bera." I punched Var in the midsection. Hard. "Her name is Bera."

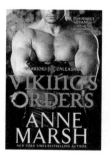 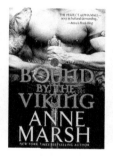 

# JOIN THE NEWSLETTER!

Want to be the first to learn about new releases and get access to special sneak peeks? Join the newsletter at
http://www.myauthorbiz.com/ENewsletter.php?acct=MM2328162713600

**If you enjoyed this story, please take a moment to post a review online and share what you enjoyed.** Many readers value the opinion of other readers like yourself. Plus, I love knowing what the "good parts" were so that I can make sure to include plenty more of them in the next book!

# ABOUT THE AUTHOR

After ten years of graduate school and too many degrees, Anne Marsh escaped to become a technical writer. When not planted firmly in front of the laptop translating Engineer into English, Anne enjoys gardening, running (even if it's just to the 7-11 for slurpees), and reading books curled up with her kids. The best part of writing romance, however, is finally being able to answer the question: "So… what do you do with a PhD in Slavic Languages and Literatures?" She lives in Northern California with her husband, two kids and four cats.

anne-marsh.com
facebook.com/annemarshauthor
@anne_marsh
goodreads.com/AnneMarsh

Printed in Great Britain
by Amazon

26695866R00101